With best wishes

from the author

Keith

The Judas Factor

A novel

Keith Sharp

Haberfield Editions

6a The Close, Holcombe

Devon EX7 0JH

United Kingdom

This book is a work of fiction. With the exception of artis such as Dali and Gauguin, and one or two dead Russians, all characters stem from the author's imagination. Van Gogh's letter to his brother Theo from Arles is the real McCoy, however, and has been well documented. The author is pleased to acknowledge Martin Bailey's *Studio in the South* as the source of the excerpt quoted in Chapter Nine.
Caravaggio's *Judith and Holofernes,* valued at more than £100 million and scheduled for auction in Toulouse in 2020,
was sold beforehand to a private buyer for an undisclosed sum.

ABOUT THE AUTHOR

Keith Sharp has published ten books, including ***You can't say that!*** and ***From Hags to Bitches,*** both of which are available on Amazon. He was born near Orpington, Kent, in 1938 and has lived in Australia, New Zealand, Canada and Libya. During National Service, he spent two years with Army Public Relations in Singapore and Hong Kong. In recent years, he has travelled extensively in South America. He currently lives in Devonshire. As a journalist, he has written for all the non-tabloid Fleet Street dailies. He was assistant City editor of the London Evening News and business editor of The Bulletin, Sydney. Long before Gaddafi appeared on the scene, he whizzed around Tripoli on his Vespa, reporting for the *Sunday Ghibli*. He has also worked for television (Channel 9, Brisbane), on a rice farm, in a uranium mine (Mary K) and as a seaman aboard a Dutch ship (the *Amstelveen)*. In 2010, he stood for Parliament as an Independent, campaigning for the restoration of civil liberties eroded by the Blair regime.

WHAT THE CRITICS SAID

...about the author's first book, The House of Mammon, published in 1971: *"Mr Sharp has a sense of humour that bubbles over at every opportunity."* – Daily Examiner, Grafton, NSW

Tell Sid to Watch it! (1987): *"Keith Sharp assumes that you have a decent level of intelligence, a dry sense of humour and a taste for good writing."* – Your Money. *"Lively and snappily written."* – The Times.

Conversations with my Broker (a novel) by Sid: *"We all remember Sid."* -- Punch. "*Genuine humour.*" -- Scottish Accountant. "*Readable and quick-witted.*" -- The Independent.

From Hags to Bitches, published on Kindle, 2014: *"Brilliant and funny ... I fell about laughing."* – Sally Porch, artist

Chapter I

KOVALSKI. That was her name. Or was it Kazinski? Guy couldn't quite remember. Something Polish, anyway. He could not even recall her first name. Sonya? Suzy, perhaps? Hardly the most promising start to an amorous adventure. He remembered the bird all right. Nice piece of work; well-stacked, neat little botty, warm, friendly eyes, not the cold, calculating type that led to heart-ache and financial stress. He'd encountered more than enough of those. No, this bird's eyes – he wished he could remember the name – put a sparkle into his own. Her make-up was subdued and understated; just a touch of mascara and a trace of lipstick. No jewellery or studs through the nose, thank goodness. A hint of some exotic and indefinable scent clung to her person. She was, he realised with a jolt, thoroughly wholesome and attractive. Just the type of woman that kept him awake at night.

They had met at a reception to launch his latest book, a graphic novel about the plunder of Jewish assets during the second world war. Missing works of art and all that. Nothing too gory. People didn't want yet another grim tale about Hitler's efforts to purify the Reich. Or how the Jews were rounded up and herded into the gas chambers, thinking they were going to have a nice shower before getting down to work. Unless they - the readers - were fascists with a political agenda of their own. The sort of people who were once again making their voices heard in Europe.

Guy had never been to Poland. Nor, it appeared, had Miss Kovalski.

"I'm a third-generation immigrant," she explained. "I'll probably be deported when Britain leaves the EU."

"I hope not," Guy replied. "On my royalties, I couldn't afford to visit you in Warsaw."

She half-turned and smiled indulgently at a man whose interest in books, Guy suspected, was probably confined to a collection of sleazy, second-hand paperbacks.

"My family came from Gdansk," she said.

Damn! thought Guy. Have I jumped the gun? One had to be so careful when making a pass these days. You could never tell how a woman would react, thanks to the virulent old biddies of the *#MeToo* brigade.

"What do you do for a living?" he asked,

"I'm...in the antiques business," she said.

"What kind of antiques?"

"Oh, anything really. Pots, paintings, bric-a-brac."

"Is that why you're here?" he asked, noting that she had barely touched her wine. "Hoping to pick up a few tips?"

"Well, I did hear that your book might contain some interesting snippets."

He laughed. "I'm afraid you're going to be very disappointed. It's fiction from start to finish."

The little man with the much-thumbed paperbacks caught her eye. He obviously fancied his chances. Guy tore himself away and mingled with the other guests. The usual crowd of deadbeats and freeloaders and blokes looking for an easy lay. They would be out of luck, he thought. Females were in short supply and those who were there looked as though they might prefer each other. So long as they gave him a good write-up, he didn't care. His thoughts were focussed on Miss Kovalski and her neat little botty.

"Kovalski?" mused his agent when Guy dropped in to discuss the launch next day. "Never heard of her."

"You invited her," said Guy.

"I did not invite her," Robert protested. "She was probably a gate-crasher."

"Birds like that don't gate-crash receptions to launch books about the Holocaust."

"You'd be surprised what some people will do for a free drink," the agent replied, glancing at the latest email. "Anyway, Kovalski is a very common name. The Polish equivalent of Smith, I believe. Trying to find her would be like looking for a needle in a haystack."

"In Poland, maybe. But not in London."

"Have you any idea how many bloody foreigners there are in London these days? You're lucky to hear English on the Tube in the morning, let alone a Cockney accent."

"Diversity, Blair called it."

"Perversity, more like it."

Guy looked out of the window. The view was impressive, if you liked that sort of thing. A sterile vista of glass and concrete, reflecting the warped egos of draftsmen with no talent and a blatant contempt for the environment. They should be forced to confront their brutality, he thought, not allowed to hide away in the country, calling themselves architects and dreaming up new ways to inflict pain on the public. He wondered how much his agent was paying for an office like this.

"Anyway, she's probably got a bloke," said Robert. "That sort of woman always has."

"I didn't notice a ring anywhere."

"That doesn't mean a thing these days. You're more likely to find a pledge of eternal love tattooed on her fanny."

"I should be so lucky."

"In any case," said Robert, "women are all the same, horizontally. Stop worrying about her. Find somebody else."

Guy suppressed a sigh. The prospect of a romantic fling was fading rapidly. He didn't know where she lived, or where she worked, or even whether her name was Kovalski. Perhaps, in the cultural desert beyond the literary circuit, inhabited by accountants and their personal assistants, she was simply Miss Smith. She probably wouldn't buy his novel, anyway. Half the bimbos he knew had never read a book in their lives. Their view of the world was shaped by Twitter and Facebook. A world of weirdos and misfits, nutters and narcissists; exactly the sort of people he tried to avoid.

Guy Chandler was a scribbler of the old school. Still only thirty-six, he was already what some people would call a young fogey. He wore a suit, read the Spectator (in the library, when he couldn't afford a copy of his own), believed in syntax, not sin, and was a stickler for punctuation. (That was one thing he had managed to learn at his minor public school.) Commas had to be in the right place while gratuitous, four-letter words had no place at all. Sex came into the same category as drugs and pornography - to be avoided unless absolutely essential. He believed a plot ought to be strong enough to carry the story without the addition of sensual fripperies.

"So it ought, old boy," said his publisher, a man whose reputation for spotting a best-seller was regarded, not least by himself, as second to none. "But just remember this: sex sells. If we don't provide it, somebody else will."

"Doesn't sound very moral to me," said Guy.

"What has morality got to do with it? We're in business to sell books, not teach archbishops how to suck eggs."

Guy conceded that he might be out of touch with the reading habits of the Great British Public. He had read somewhere that most best-sellers made the list without a single bodice being ripped. Either he or the publisher had got it wrong.

"How do you think it will go?" he asked.

"How will what go?"

"The Cartesian triangle."

"Who knows?" the publisher shrugged. "Probably sell a few thousand. If we're lucky."

A few thousand, thought Guy. That might just be enough to buy a ticket to Warsaw, even if it would not allow him to put down a deposit on a yacht. It might not even buy Miss Kaminski, or whatever she called herself, a decent meal. Provided he could find her and she didn't already have a bloke.

Strange, he thought, that he had not come across the name before, especially if it was as common as Robert had suggested. Not that he had done much by way of research; fiction, after all, required imagination, not a recital of historical facts. Just enough to give the plot credibility and show that the author was not an ignorant hill-billy. He did not go in for secret codes or, heaven forbid!, mirror writing and other hackneyed devices. Anybody – except, perhaps, a few demented Holocaust deniers – who didn't know that Auschwicz was a byword for evil would be better off with an Enid Blyton. And even she was suspect in an era of political correctness. He decided that, once the dust had settled, he would try to seek her out. He would, as the police might say, make a few enquiries.

He was also vaguely disturbed by the news from Poland. The Poles were a bit touchy about Auschwicz these days. Anyone would think it was they who had built the ovens that reduced a million Jews, gypsies and transvestites to a few sacks of bone meal. The government was even threatening unspecified sanctions against anybody who referred to 'Polish death camps'. Guy regarded that as not only an attack on free speech but as yet another attempt to rewrite history. If Auschwicz wasn't in Poland, where was it? He was determined to resist such pressure and was glad that his own publisher, unlike some who had kowtowed to the tyrants in Peking, thought likewise. But for how long, he wondered? When profits were at stake, principles tended to fly out of the window.

Guy returned to his flat in Blackheath, both anxious and depressed. The excitement generated by the publication of his first novel some years ago had long since given way to nervous anticipation. Pre-publication blues, he called them, on a par with the anguish suffered by women about to give birth. Would the new arrival bring pleasure or be a continual source of maternal angst? On this occasion, the blues were exacerbated by a mystery woman who had turned up at the launch party and dominated his thoughts ever since. Even fogeys were not immune to the demands of the flesh.

He did not really like living south of the river but could not afford anywhere decent further north. Rents in Hampstead and thereabouts were not only beyond his reach but quite exorbitant. He had often thought the answer to the housing shortage might be to reopen one or two death camps, in Poland or anywhere else, specifically for estate agents and *rentiers*. If a handful of latter-day Rachmans could be thrown in for good measure, he would volunteer to stoke the furnaces himself. On the other hand, he did not want to live among the so-called literati who infested the fashionable suburbs to the north and amused themselves by stabbing each other in the back. He preferred his critics to be out in the open. And there were enough of those, north and south of the river.

He looked in the fridge for something to eat. The search was short and unrewarding. Some cold sausage left over from breakfast two days ago, a bowl of grapefruit that had seen better days and a tin of baked beans. What were they doing in the fridge? It was at times like this that he really wished he had a woman in the house. She would ensure that he had something proper to eat, not leftovers from the day before. Were such thoughts unworthy of a writer who believed in equality? What if they were? He needed a woman about the place, and not just for stocking the fridge.

His thoughts returned to Miss Kovalski. Was she, he wondered, the sort of Pole who ate gherkins for breakfast? He was once beguiled by a young lady from Serbia who kept a jar at her bedside. Pickled cucumbers at eight o'clock in the morning were not conducive to romance. Nor, for that matter, were baked beans. A gentleman, he had constantly to remind himself, did not eat baked beans, at breakfast or at any other time. He poured some oil – why did they call it extra virgin when, once the bottle had been opened, the seal was no longer intact? – into the frying pan, slit the sausages down the middle and watched them sizzle gently. He found a tomato, cut it in half and threw it into the pan. Might as well get rid of the beans, he thought, opening the can pouring half the contents into a saucepan. He wondered why people thought authors were rich. Most teetered on the brink of starvation, like actors in some long-forgotten repertory company.

His thoughts were interrupted by the telephone in the hall. A journalist wanting a few words before publication, perhaps? A spot of additional publicity was always useful, like an extra virgin in

Paradise. He was about to pick up the handset when he remembered the sausages. Returning to the kitchen, he turned off the heat and hurried back to the hall. As he reached the phone, the ringing stopped.

"Blast!" he exclaimed. "I bet they've withheld their number."

He was right. They had. At least it would save him the cost of ringing back. He returned to the kitchen, tipped the beans into the frying pan and gave everything a good stir. They'd all get mixed up in his stomach, so what the hell?

He wondered who might be calling at this hour. The book was not due out until the day after tomorrow, so it could not have been a breathless fan dying to tell him how good it was, or even a bookseller demanding to know when the author might turn up to sign a few copies. Guy had a stock answer for booksellers of this ilk, the sort of answer that could be found among those gratuitous expletives not deleted from the pages of books by less punctilious authors. Could it, he wondered hopefully, have been the woman who had occupied his thoughts for the past day or two? If so, how could she have obtained his number? Like many people who regarded themselves a cut above the common herd, Guy was ex-directory. Even his email address was not publicised. But, as he was the first to acknowledge, nothing was secret in the world of cyberspace. One did not have to work for GCHQ to know that. For a hundred quid, you could obtain not only the phone number but the home address, marital status, criminal record and even the sexual proclivities of just about anybody on the planet. The phone-hacking scandal that had engulfed the News of the World had made that all too clear. Privacy was a thing of the past.

Oh, well, whoever it was would no doubt phone back. He just hoped it wasn't the bank manager, wanting to exact more blood for exceeding his overdraft limit. He might write a book about these shysters one day. Perhaps reserve them a seat in the tumbrel taking the Rachmans to the gas chamber. That should make him some new friends and help to sell a few books. He might even be accused of anti-Semitism, proving he was not so out of touch, after all.

Chapter II

Guy was pleased with the generally favourable reviews of *The Cartesian triangle.* Nothing that would catapult him into the best-seller lists but at least none of the critics had torn it to shreds. Even the disciples of Sappho had been generous with their praise. The only sour note was struck by a writer on an obscure magazine who clearly had an axe to grind. Had he been paid to stick the knife in, Guy wondered, or was he just one of those pathetic souls who cruised the internet looking for somebody on whom to vent their spleen? In any event, it was patently obvious that he had not read the book.

As he toured the radio stations in London and the Home Counties, Guy thought of the royalties that might accrue to help keep the wolf from the door. He was even interviewed on the BBC World Service which he hoped might lead to an offer of translation. Polish, French, Serbo-Croat? Who could say? These were early days and he had learned not to pitch his hopes too high. The road to bankruptcy was littered with the forlorn pages of remaindered copies.

He had almost forgotten Miss Kovalski during the hectic few days on the promotional trail. Not entirely, of course, because her image was embedded too firmly in his mind. Was she really just a freeloader, one of those bimbos who turned up at various functions, smiled at the doorman, nibbled the canapés, sampled the wine and then departed, never to be seen again? He hoped not. Something about her told him she was not simply one of those ships that passed in the night. For a moment, he even sniffed danger in the air. He could not say why but his intuition seldom let him down.

One morning, when at last he had some time to call his own, he caught the train from Blackheath to London Bridge. The City always quickened his pulse, even more so now that most of the cowboys had departed for Canary Wharf, a few hundred yards downstream. The Square Mile somehow retained an air of probity, despite all the crooks and kleptocrats still domiciled there. Many of their predecessors, captured in oils by artists also long dead, beamed down from the walls of boardrooms across the City. Many were Jews, others eminent Quakers; nearly all were notable old rogues, not above pulling a fast one to make a few quid. Guy marvelled at how many of the portraits had survived the Blitz. They had obviously been spirited away to the country for safe keeping as German bombs rained down on the capital. Had the Nazis managed to cross the Channel, one or two might well have featured in *The Cartesian triangle*.

The street names which gave the Square Mile much of its character appealed to his sense of history. The streets themselves might no longer be paved with gold – Swiss francs and the Japanese yen had long ago pushed that barbarous relic to the margins of credibility – but they still resonated with the wealth of ages past. Lombard Street, home of Italian bankers (not the sort found hanging under Blackfriars Bridge); Leadenhall Market, so named because of all the lead on the roof. Poultry, the Old Jewry, both self-explanatory. Gresham Street, named after the man who said bad money drove out the good. How much more romantic they all were than Canary Wharf which had risen Phoenix-like from the rubble of the Isle of Dogs.

He decided to cross the river on foot, gazing down at the murky waters below. No self-respecting salmon could possibly live in this sludge, let alone a whale, unless it was stoned on all the cocaine flushed down the nation's loos. Even with a few tame oysters to filter the worst of the goo it was not the sort of stream in which one would care to swim very far. At least it wasn't the Ganges, the Hindu version of a lethal injection. He turned into Cannon Street, then made his way up Cheapside towards the Guildhall. As a journalist, he had once dined there, exchanging views with aldermen (and women) over lemon sole and apricot crumble, while on the streets outside, protesters angered by greed and globalisation clashed with the City's very own police force. The protesters had gone but the greed remained. The City was now awash with Russian money, corrupting all who came into contact with it. Even the most respectable banks were now apparently in the laundry business. Gresham's Law all over again.

Guy suspected that on this occasion he might well be on a fool's errand. The Guildhall's library dealt mainly with business and finance. The staff were unlikely to have much sympathy for a middle-aged bloke looking for a needle in a haystack. A Polish haystack, at that.

"Have you tried the internet?" asked the harassed matron in charge of the enquiries desk, peering at him through her bifocals.

"I'm not too clued up about that sort of thing," said Guy, conveniently forgetting the computer in his study. "I'm an author, not a technocrat."

"What sort of books do you write?" the librarian asked, trying to conceal her interest. She had dealt with authors before and knew that a simple enquiry could lead to hours of painstaking research, time that could be better spent on other matters.

"I'm sure you've heard of my latest, *The Cartesian triangle.* It's only just come out."

"Oh, so you wrote that, did you? I'm afraid we've decided not to stock it."

"Life is full of surprises," said Guy.

"If people want to read that sort of stuff, they can buy a copy of their own."

"I quite agree," said Guy.

The woman signalled to one of her colleagues, a haughty bitch who looked as though ice wouldn't melt in her mouth. Probably a man-hater, thought Guy, a graduate of some red-brick university out of her depth in the City where a little bit of class still went a long way.

"Would you please show this gentleman how to search the internet? He has apparently just emerged from the Dark Ages."

She returned to her work, which apparently involved stapling sheets of A4 together, while Guy followed the ice-maiden to the bank of computers. A dozen or so other people were already seated, eyes glued to the screen while manipulating their mouse.

"Just type in what you want to know and follow the instructions," the bitch said. "If it's there, you'll find it."

"Thank you so much," said Guy. "I don't know why I didn't

think of it before."

He sat down and wondered where to begin. Perhaps it would be easier just to browse through the printed matter on the shelves first. He had spent many hours thumbing through ancient, often decaying, volumes in libraries here and there. Many of these were now available online, of course, provided one knew where to look. But somehow a computer didn't have quite the same feel as a leather-bound volume with printed pages. He could understand why people still preferred 'proper' books to electronic platforms, such as Kindle.

He typed in the word Kovalski. He might just as well not have bothered. So what about Poland? No, that was far too sweeping. He'd be inundated with everything from Chopin to the Munich agreement. He could do without a treatise on the composer's affaire with George Sand. Besides, he had no wish to be reminded that she was a lot more successful than he could ever hope to be. Munich? That was nearer the mark. It was Chamberlain's much-derided assertion that he had negotiated "peace for our time" that had led to the discovery of all those death camps on Polish soil. And without the war, and the plunder it begat, he could not have written *The Cartesian triangle*. He supposed he ought to be grateful to the man excoriated for failing to call Hitler's bluff.

Miss Kovalski claimed she was a third-generation immigrant. Many Poles did settle in Britain after serving with the Allied forces. Her grandfather may well have been among them. Others fled when the communists seized control. He tried 'Polish communities in Britain'

The response was immediate and overwhelming. Good old Google! Now he was getting somewhere. Among the torrent of words, he noted there were Polish communities in several towns. Some were recent, triggered by Poland's accession to the Treaty of Rome, others more established. But England was a big place and he could not visit them all. He racked his brain for a clue. Where might she have been born? Her voice, of course! No trace of flat, northern vowels and certainly not of Scottish ones. Her accent pointed to the southern counties of England, his own stomping ground.

A reference to a Polish community in Devon aroused his interest. Many Poles, it seemed, had settled near Newton Abbot, wherever that was. For some reason, he thought of horses, then remembered the racing tips he heard on the *Today* programme every morning. Guy was not interested in horses, or betting. He barely knew one end of a horse from the other and had never been a gambler. He had bought tickets in the office sweepstake, of course, but just to be matey. Once, he had even drawn the winner of the Grand National. But that was only because the favourite had fallen and broken its neck.

Despite his current status as self-employed, at least in the eyes of the Inland Revenue, Guy had once worked in an office. In several, actually. He had begun his career as a junior hack on some provincial newspaper, the title of which he now preferred to forget. He had done his share of foot-in-the-door interviews with people who didn't want to be interviewed. Once or twice, he had been threatened with violence while investigating some dodgy scam. By the time he was ready for a job in Fleet Street, Fleet Street had gone down the can, devoured by technology and usurped by the internet. The once-great newspapers that had kept the nation informed were now dispersed across the capital, more interested in survival than veracity. Many lesser titles, magazines as well as newspapers, had yielded to economic pressure and called it a day. The blogosphere reigned supreme. Guy retreated to the suburbs and turned his pen towards fiction. He ditched his jeans, bought a suit and cultivated the persona of a man of literature. So far, it had worked. At least, he no longer had to worry about deadlines and the ever-present threat of libel.

Suddenly he thought: what the hell am I doing here, in the Guildhall, looking for a bimbo who was probably masquerading under a false name and had a bloke, anyway? He was just being silly, like the besotted old fool in Maugham's *Of Human Bondage.* Miss Kovalski was becoming an obsession, an *idée fixe* that precluded progress elsewhere. But why, he asked himself, should he be ashamed of his feelings? Had not Dr Freud warned against bottling up the emotions? The British were far too uptight, especially about sex, which is why so many of them ended up in the nuthouse. He decided there and then to save the NHS a bit of money and follow his instinct. He would go to Newton Abbot and pursue his enquiries. At least it would get him out of town and help him to relax after his gruelling tour of radio and TV stations.

He left the Guildhall, more than ever aware of the dull ache in his chest and the familiar sensation in his loins. Sexual desire was not just a device for spicing up the pages of some dreary novel. It was a vital force, the mainspring of life. Dr Freud, he concluded, knew what he was talking about.

Chapter III

The first shock was to discover the price of a ticket to Newton Abbot. He was not working for a newspaper now and could not claim the fare on expenses. The money came straight out of his own pocket. Brunel, who had built the Great Western Railway, would have been appalled by the cost of rail travel, the highest in Europe. He had wanted his railway to open up the country, not force travellers into bankruptcy. Guy was not surprised to see so few other passengers, even in second class. He shuddered to think how much a first-class ticket would have set him back. And the fare did not even include lunch, just a packet of crisps if you were lucky.

The railways had always captured Guy's imagination. They were the bedrock of civilisation, impressive feats of engineering that carried ideas, as well as goods, to remote towns and villages. From the jungles of South America to the steppes of Siberia, they had changed the way people lived. Sadly, many of them – the Hejaz railway across the desert in Saudi Arabia; the single, narrow-gauge line over the Andes – had either been destroyed by war (Lawrence had done his best to wreck the Hejaz) or succumbed to progress. There was still much to impress, however, including the huge, powerful locomotives that hauled passengers and freight across America. Dozens of songs had been written about them: the Chattanooga choo-choo – the lyrics now censored to appease the p.c. lobby – as well as a little ditty he particularly liked about the Atchison, Topeka and Santa Fe line, which straddled several states in the south-west. Guy had been to Santa Fe in Argentina but there were no railways there. There had been but, like much else in that unhappy country, they had collapsed through corruption and mismanagement.

His grandfather had once shown him a picture of what he called the graveyard of the giants in Zagreb, Yugoslavia. Hundreds of huge, fire-eating locos, now woefully out of steam, had been left to rot in the marshalling yard, like elephants waiting to die in the African bush. Some of them, he now realised, must have had a less-than-illustrious career. They, along with the dozens of smaller, pocket-sized engines rusting quietly next to them, had almost certainly been used to transport Jews to the death camps in Poland and elsewhere. The man who organised it all, Adolf Eichmann, was later tracked down to Argentina, not a million miles from Santa Fe.

The trolley approached – he let it pass – as the train glided effortlessly through the countryside. He had no wish to be ripped off for a cup of coffee that would probably have been undrinkable, anyway. They were travelling at well over a hundred miles an hour, so why the rush to build HS2? This was fast enough for most mortal beings. The only people to benefit from such a project would be a handful of businessmen who could afford the fare and reach their destinations nine and a half minutes earlier. But at what cost to the taxpayer and the environment? Guy could understand why Mr Lud occupied so much space in the history books.

They were somewhere in Wiltshire. But where? Guy couldn't say. He'd seen a white horse along the way but that meant nothing. It wasn't even a real horse, just a bit of ancient graffiti, carved out of chalk. He closed his eyes and dozed off, oblivious of the CCTV cameras overhead, watching him even as he slept.

"The next stop will be Tiverton Parkway," announced a well-rounded female voice over the tannoy. "Will passengers..."

The recording was abruptly cut short and superseded by the coarse tones of the guard. "We'll be arriving at Tiverton in about four minutes. Will customers please ensure they have all their baggage before alighting? Thank you for travelling Great Western."

Guy had only one small suitcase and wasn't getting off, anyway. Can't be far now, he thought. He looked at the map Mr Brunel's successors had kindly provided. Two or three stops, that's all. Another profitable trip for the company whose directors paid themselves huge salaries but were unable to make the trains run on time. Brunel's atmospheric railway between Exeter and Newton Abbot had been destroyed by rats which gnawed away at the leather fittings. Now the railways were being eroded by rodents of a different kind. The new breed of robber barons, who lined their pockets with money that could be used to build a better railway, would make ideal candidates for the gas chambers, alongside the Rachmans and *rentiers* already in the tumbrels.

The train pulled into Exeter St. David's. Here were signs of progress, as befitted the home of the Met. Office. The joint had literary connections, too. Guy recalled that Allen Lane had founded his publishing empire after failing to find anything worth reading on this very station. Had the Romans not thrown in the towel after building their wall, the city might have been the capital of England. *Dum albion*, they called it. It even had a university. If he had time, he would stop on the way home and perhaps visit the cathedral. Pity that houses were so expensive; on a par with London, the overcrowded and far less scenic metropolis to the east.

The guard's whistle blew. Doors slammed. Next stop, he thought, as the train began to move. He felt a surge of anticipation, muted only by a pang of doubt, as it picked up speed. Was he being foolish or was this the start of a true adventure? Everybody needed an adventure now and again. Guy felt sorry for those who put security first and had never experienced the thrill of the chase. As Nietzsche said, to get the most out of life, one had to live dangerously. For Paraguayans celebrating the inaugural run of the country's first steam train, that meant a close encounter of the apocalyptic kind. They were given a tantalising glimpse of eternity when the train failed to stop at the end of the line and careered into the jungle. Why spoil the fun for want of a few yards of track? Dr. Beeching could not have arranged matters with more panache.

There were no such thrills for those aboard Great Western's service from Paddington to Penzance. The train continued its journey along the River Exe, running so close to the sea that Guy could almost taste the salt. Dozens of boats, large and small, lay peacefully at anchor, unruffled by the tide. Did anybody live on them or were they the nautical version of second homes? Maybe they were just on standby for the Coast Guard, waiting to rescue a few illegal migrants trying to cross the Channel on inflatable dinghies. In days of old, when smugglers ruled the waves, a few of the larger vessels would probably have given Customs officers a run for their money. The train sped on, affording a fleeting glimpse of a small station called Starcross. Not the most auspicious omen for somebody in search of romance.

He realised he must be nearing his destination when the racetrack hove into view. Next meeting: . Just a blank space where the date ought to have been. A chance to use the ground for a quick game of polo, perhaps, or possibly a car-boot sale. He noticed some people dragging brushwood jumps into place, so maybe the next meeting wasn't far off. He must listen out for the racing tips on the *Today* programme. Perhaps even have a flutter. The train pulled into the station. Guy shouldered his bag and stepped on to the platform.

A recorded message designed to induce paranoia boomed out of the void. "Please do not leave your luggage unattended," it warned. "Unattended bags may be taken away and destroyed."

Welcome to Newton Abbot, thought Guy.

During its heyday, the town must have been an impressive place, full of steam and smoke, including some from Brunel's cigar. The famous photograph of the engineer, top-hatted and with cigar in hand, always reminded him of Winston Churchill. Unlike Exeter, large parts of which had been destroyed by the Luftwaffe, Newton Abbot had survived the war more or less intact. The enemy was once more at the gates, however, attacking under a different guise. The railway workshops, where trains from all over the region once came to be serviced and repaired, had long since been demolished. In their place stood a collection of nondescript warehouses. Even now, a bulldozer was preparing the ground for another development. Probably a supermarket, thought Guy, to help put more small shopkeepers out of business. A quick glance up the main street showed why Miss Kovalski had sought the bright lights of London. Apathy and neglect shrieked from the shop fronts.

"Taxi?" cried one of the drivers parked hopefully in the station forecourt.

"Do you know of a decent hotel?" Guy asked, noticing that one opposite had been boarded up.

"I can take you to an hotel, mate," the driver said, "but whether it's decent or not I wouldn't like to say."

"So long as it's clean and not too expensive," said Guy.

"Hop in."

Guy put his bag on the back seat and, seized by sudden burst of fraternity, as well as a desire to prise what information he could out of the driver, sat next to him in front.

"I believe there was a Polish community here at one stage," he ventured as they drove through town.

"That's right. Out near Trago Mills. An old people's home now, I think. Want me to take you there?"

"Not at the moment," said Guy hurriedly. "Tomorrow, maybe."

They passed a sign directing them to Decoy country park. What a peculiar name! thought Guy. He hoped it wasn't a metaphor for this entire exercise. Was he walking into a trap, with Miss Kovalski used as bait?

"Here you are, mate," the driver said, pulling into the courtyard of a small bed-and-breakfast establishment. "They'll look after you. Plenty of room this time of year. Not many punters stay overnight, anyway."

The hotel was pleasingly compact. It reminded him of the *hostals* he had stayed at in South America. Small, bright, comfortable and not too far off the beaten track. If there were any other guests, they were keeping a low profile.

"Will you be wanting an evening meal, sir?" asked the owner, a wizened old man who looked as though, like the candle in that American woman's poem, he might not last the night.

"If it won't put you to any trouble," said Guy.

"No trouble at all, sir. But I'm afraid it will have to be table d'hôte."

"Whatever's going," said Guy, surprised to hear such a phrase in an age of take-aways and instant noodles. He hoped the meal would be something more substantial than a slice of pizza and a bit of salad.

He unpacked and made himself a cup of tea, then lay down on the bed. What the hell, he asked himself yet again, am I doing here? I must be an utter fool! Why not spend a week or so in Tangier or the Azores and relax in style? A bit of sunshine and a bowl of gazpacho would do more to help him unwind than a few days on the trail of an elusive bimbo in the West Country. Probably be a lot cheaper, too. The fare from Paddington to Newton Abbot still rankled.

As he gazed at the ceiling, thinking of date palms and blue skies, his eyes wandered to an old photograph on the wall. The sepia print showed an airman, complete with goggles and flying jacket, waving from the cockpit of an ancient fighter plane. Guy knew no more about planes than he did about horses, so it might have been a Spitfire or a Hurricane. He knew it wasn't Concorde. The plane sported British markings – the roundels were clearly visible – although something about the pilot suggested foreign blood. Guy sat up and studied the picture carefully.

"That old photo in my room," he said as the proprietor served dinner. "When was that taken?"

"I think you must be referring to the photo of my grandfather, sir," said the old man, placing a large tureen on the table. "He served with the Royal Air Force during the war."

"*With* the Royal Air Force?"

"Yes, sir. He was a member of the Polish resistance before he escaped to England and joined up."

The Polish resistance! So, he was on the right track, even at this early stage. He wished he had given the taxi driver a bigger tip.

"He's been dead a good many years, I imagine?"

"I'm afraid so. My father, too. I sometimes think it won't be long before I join them."

He smiled wanly, as though apologising for his advancing years.

"What did your father do?" asked Guy, removing the lid of the tureen and discovering an entire meal.

"He ran a little shop. Quite successful it was, too, until the supermarkets came along."

"The customers then drifted away, I suppose?"

"I wouldn't say drifted, sir. They deserted us, heading for the special offers and Green Shield stamps as fast as their legs could carry them."

"Yes, the supermarkets have a lot to answer for," said Guy, realising he had touched a raw nerve. "Unfortunately, they are what people seem to want."

"I shop at one myself," the old man said. "I even have a loyalty card."

Guy swallowed a mouthful of soup – home-made, by the taste of it, with more than a hint of beetroot – and said: "I suppose you've never come across the name Kovalski?"

The proprietor smiled.

"That's a very common name in Poland, sir. There must have been quite a few of them around here at one stage. They've all moved on, one way or another."

He stepped back respectfully from the table and said: "Don't let your soup get cold, sir. I'll have a think while you sup."

Guy saw no more of the old man until breakfast the following morning. He had slept well, undisturbed by thoughts of either Miss Kovalski or the long-dead Polish pilot who shared the room with him. He made his way to the dining room, prepared for a long – and probably frustrating – day among the byways of Devon.

"I've had a word with some friends of mine," the proprietor said, setting down Guy's eggs and bacon. "They may be able to help, but there's no guarantee."

"Any information would be more than welcome. When can I meet them?"

"As it happens, they're coming into town today to do some shopping."

"Not at the supermarket, I hope?" said Guy, instantly biting his tongue.

"I expect so," the old man replied, apparently unfazed. "But they can call in here, if you like, and you can have a chat."

"I'd like that very much. Are they Polish, by the way?"

"The man's parents were; his wife's Czech."

"Please tell them I'd love to meet them."

With an hour to kill before they arrived, Guy explored the nearby lanes. Rural suburbia, he decided. Not exactly Blackheath but pleasant enough. The houses were well-spaced, a mixture of old and new. Two horses that looked as though they were destined for the knacker's yard grazed peacefully in a small field. The glue factory rather than a French restaurant, he fancied. In the distance, he could just see what he assumed were the crags of Dartmoor. A few wisps of white cloud drifted lazily over the summit. A helicopter, probably the air ambulance, whirred past. Otherwise nothing disturbed the tranquillity of this rustic retreat. The more he thought about it, the more he wondered why he lived in London, with its high rents and dangerous levels of air pollution. Down here, the air actually tasted different. He filled his lungs and felt invigorated.

At eleven o'clock, he returned to his lodgings and was walking up the drive when a mud-spattered Land Rover drew up beside him. The driver waved and wound down the window.

"Mr Chandler? I'm Chris Lopata. I hear you'd like a chat?"

"If it's not inconvenient."

"Not at all."

Chris Lopata may have been Polish but he was every inch a Devon farmer. His dark, wavy hair was turning grey and he had the open, honest face of a countryman. His handshake made Guy wince. He parked the wagon and introduced his wife, a jolly, buxom woman with slightly Slavonic cheekbones and a friendly smile.

"My wife, Alena," he said. "Let's go inside," he added, leading the way.

The old man had laid out a table and was already waiting with a pot of coffee. The four of them sat down.

"Tomasz" – the farmer nodded towards the proprietor – "tells me that you are trying to trace the Kovalskis?"

"Just one of them, actually. A young lady..."

The trio hooted with laughter.

"I might have guessed there was a woman involved," chortled Chris. "There always is."

"Don't get me wrong," said Guy hurriedly, trying to hide his embarrassment. "I'm an author and I need some information."

"Well, that's a new one!" Alena exclaimed. "At least you're not trying to track down a long-lost aunt who has left you a fortune."

"That's my next project," said Guy, provoking another guffaw.

The old man poured the coffee and offered Guy a biscuit.

"Are you writing a book about them?" he asked.

"Not exactly," said Guy, wondering how much to tell them. "I'm following up one I've already written."

"I knew the family quite well," said Alena. "They used to attend mass – when they felt like it or needed to get something off their chest."

"They were Catholics?"

"Of course. Most Poles are."

"The Jews were nearly all wiped out," said Chris. "Those who didn't go up in smoke mostly emigrated."

"Was it a large family?" asked Guy.

"There were three girls," Alena told him. "One died, one married and went to America, the other just disappeared."

"Disappeared?"

"Yeah," said Chris. "I wasn't sorry to see her go. Always poking her nose into other people's business. A real pain in the arse."

"Now, darling! Remember you're not in the cowshed now."

"Sorry, mein liebes."

"Can you remember her name?" asked Guy.

"Lucy, I think. Something like that."

Lucy, of course! Not Suzy. Lucy Kovalski: the words had a nice mellifluous ring to them.

"And she just disappeared?"

"Without a trace. Somebody told me she had joined the police force."

"The police?"

Guy was so shocked that he spilt his coffee. He was none too fond of the police whom he regarded as petty tyrants with an inflated idea of their own importance. As a reporter on that now defunct provincial newspaper, he had seen them at work, often using strong-arm tactics to arrest demonstrators but apparently unable to catch any criminals.

"Yeah. That would be right up her street. Always sniffing around where she wasn't wanted."

Guy felt quite ill. How could he have failed to see that she was no more an antiques dealer than he was archbishop of Canterbury? Since quitting his job as a journalist, he seemed to have lost the ability to detect when somebody was spinning a yarn. He had become less sceptical, more willing to believe the first story he heard. His new role as a novelist didn't help. Fiction was now his stock-in-trade. He began to realise that he may have embarked not on a romantic adventure but on an exercise in futility. He had wasted a lot of time, as well as money, on what was beginning to look like a wild goose chase. He did not want to end up chasing the fuzz.

"Do you know which force she joined?" he managed to ask.

"I think it might have been Thames Valley," Alena said, "but she could be in the FBI now, for all I know. It was a long time ago."

Thames Valley was not a force that ranked highly in Guy's estimation. Too many bad apples and no respect for civil liberties. He wondered if they were talking about the same woman.

"How would you describe her?" he asked.

"Quite attractive," said Chris. "Trim little figure, nice boobs."

"Not as nice as mine," his wife contended, smacking him playfully on the wrist.

"Of course not, my love. Or Daisy's."

"Who's Daisy?" asked Guy.

"His favourite Friesian," Alena replied. "We're dairy farmers."

"Four legs and five tits," said Chris. "I had to have one of them cut off."

"Legs – or tits?" Guy found himself saying.

The old man slapped his leg and doubled up with laughter. The farmer choked on his biscuit.

"A three-legged cow with five tits!" he exclaimed. "That ought to turn a few heads at Smithfield!"

Guy realised there was more to farming than met the eye of a young fogey from Blackheath. He should have ditched the Spectator and read the Farmers' Weekly before coming to Devon.

"One thing I do remember," said Chris when the mirth had subsided. "She never missed a country-house sale or an auction. Always hanging around, looking for a bargain."

"What sort of bargain?" asked Guy. Most of his own paintings had come from local charity shops. Prints by and large but none the worse for that.

"Pictures, old porcelain, that sort of stuff. Anything arty. She went to the Steiner school at Dartington, I think. Picked up some fancy ideas there." He paused. "I don't know if she ever made any money out of it."

"What about her parents?"

"Gone the way of all flesh, I'm afraid."

The woman finished her coffee and looked at her watch. "We must be getting along, too," she said. "The milk lorry won't wait, even for Daisy."

Guy accompanied them to the Land Rover and cautiously offered his hand. "Thank you for sparing the time," he said. "I'm much obliged."

"My pleasure," replied Chris. "And remember: never trust a copper. They'll shop you as soon as look at you."

Guy was tempted to return to London by the next train. The trip had been a complete waste of time, the consequence of a young fogey's conceit and desire for a bit of skirt. He was nevertheless in no hurry to breathe the polluted air of London again. He decided to stay an extra day and explore Dartmoor. He had never been on the moor; the nearest he had come was Conan Doyle's *The Hound of the Baskervilles*. Now, according to the newspapers, some big cats – lynxes, or possibly leopards -- were said to lurk among the bushes and rocky outcrops. Products of a feverish imagination, more likely, despite the 'evidence' of some grainy photographs. Lots of ponies, though, as well as deer. They were real enough, as were the sheep killed by dogs allowed to run wild on the moor.

It had been a long time since Guy ventured beyond the literary bubble of the metropolis. Too long; life in London, with its congestion and constant surveillance, stifled creativity. He needed a change of scene to stimulate the imagination. He caught a bus, revelling in the journey through narrow country lanes where tractors – agricultural, not the Chelsea variety -- obviously had the right of way. Twice the driver found himself trapped behind one, unable to overtake. Guy could see why Daphne du Maurier and the Christie woman had lived in this part of the world. The scenery alone generated ideas. Significantly, both writers had houses on the banks of rivers. They could stop and stare and observe life as it ebbed and flowed. That was surely preferable to a dash across London in a crowded Tube. Times had changed since Dr Johnson's day.

The bus arrived at Princetown, a granite-like outpost of stark practicality eclipsed by the brooding presence of Dartmoor Prison. Over the years, some of the country's most notorious criminals had served their time there. Many had died within its walls, some as a result of the floggings they had received. The jail's infamous flogging machine was as notorious as the convicts themselves. The graveyard told a depressing story.

In its early days, the jail had been used to house prisoners of war captured during various battles with France and America. At one time, no fewer than 12,000 men were crammed into a space designed for a few hundred. Guy did not envy them. During the first world war, conscientious objectors deprived of their liberty were banged up there.

At least they had been allowed to wear their own clothes. Guy had seen pictures of them exercising in the yard, clad in pre-war civvies. These days, they would probably have been fitted out, at public expense, with prison rags and electronic tags.

He found a pub and ordered a glass of beer and a sandwich. Devon innkeepers had nothing to learn from their London counterparts, he reflected, as he pocketed the change from a £10 note. He took his lunch into the garden and sat at one of the rough-hewn wooden tables overlooking the moor. In the distance, the coastline was clearly visible. On a clear day you could probably see for ever. At night, provided there was no fog or clouds, the view of the heavens must have been spectacular. Guy wondered if the prisoners could see the stars from their cells. He had travelled half way up a mountain in Chile to look at the planets through a telescope. The view from the moor was a lot cheaper, if one discounted the beer.

Had Miss Kovalski ever walked among these green (thanks to the bracken that grew everywhere) and windswept hills? Almost certainly, as she was born just down the road. Had she, perhaps, even stopped at this very pub for a glass of ale at the end of a hot summer's day? He tried to reconcile the farmer's description of her with his own recollection of an attractive young woman. A pain in the arse, always poking her nose into other people's business. That's not how he remembered her but at least it might explain her presence at his launch party.

Chapter IV

Guy decided not to stop at Exeter on the way back. The cathedral could wait for another day. After the events in Salisbury, he did not want to be mistaken for a one-man Russian hit squad. Besides, he was anxious to return home. He felt the need to lie down, preferably in a dark room, and consider his next move. He was suffering as only a young fogey can suffer when the prospect of an exciting new romance turns to dust.

The train sped through Tiverton Parkway, not stopping this time, and raced back towards London. Taunton, Castle Cary and the Heathrow traffic came and went. Poor Queen, he thought. All those aeroplanes disturbing her little doggies. As if she hadn't got enough to worry about, what with the old boy and his bladder and the youngsters still grieving over their mother's infidelity. At Paddington, he took the Tube to Waterloo, then caught the suburban train to Blackheath.

He sensed that something was wrong the moment he walked up the path. Nothing tangible but intuition pointed towards mischief. There were no signs of forced entry, no damaged lock, no broken glass. As far as he knew, only the landlord had a duplicate key. Unless Guy had misjudged him, he was unlikely to have abused the privilege. But that somebody had been in the flat he was in no doubt. Two letters lay on the doormat. Guy picked them up and put them on his desk. A quick shufti revealed everything to be in place. Nothing missing, yet he was sure that somebody, maybe more than one person, had been poking around. His nostrils, always sensitive to unusual odours, detected the smell of a stranger. Male or female? Hard to say. If it were a woman, she wouldn't make a very good mistress. Scent, like lipstick, tended to give the game away.

He made himself a coffee, proper stuff, with beans, and sat down at his desk. Nothing missing or out of place there, either. What sort of intruder would break in and not steal anything? While MI5 had bugged and burgled its way across London in years gone by (the *Spycatcher* man had blown the gaff about that), Guy posed no threat to national security. He was not even a blogger trying to overthrow the government. Certainly not a member of an organised crime gang. So why should anyone want to break in and snoop around? It didn't make sense. Unless they wanted to plant a bug, of course.

He thought of his computer. With a deft movement of his left hand, he assured himself that the memory stick was in place and in the right port. That meant nothing, of course. The intruder could have brought his – or her – own device and downloaded all his files in a matter of seconds. He tried to think what was on them; the manuscript of *The Cartesian triangle,* a few personal letters and the current state of his bank account. Nothing too embarrassing, revealing a secret life as a train spotter or transvestite with a penchant for wearing ex-Army boots. He had not even written to Chelsea Manning. Of course, one didn't have to break in to steal the contents of a computer these days. Thanks to Edward Snowden, he was all too aware of the threat to privacy posed by GCHQ and the NSA. Nothing was safe from the prying eyes of the state.

But why would the state be interested in a virtually unknown author trying to make a name for himself in Blackheath? It could have been for one reason only: his recent book about the Holocaust. What had he written that was so interesting that somebody was prepared to break in and search his flat? His mind raced over the plot. Bloke tracks down missing picture by well-known artist. *Girl with earthenware jar* stolen by Gestapo and kept in secret location. Discovered by accident long after the war during renovation of old farmhouse near Grenoble. Hardly in same class as Monet's water lilies or Constable's haystacks. Not even listed among works of art looted by Nazis. After much kerfuffle, returned to rightful owner – or, rather, his descendants. End of story. Fiction throughout. Where's the beef?

Guy stood up and paced nervously about the room. It would have been better if somebody *had* broken in, stolen a few valuables (not that he had anything worth stealing) and made off. He felt violated, defiled by person or persons unknown. How had they known the flat was empty, anyway? Were they watching, like Big Brother? If so, where from? There were no spy cameras in the vicinity, at least none that he knew of. Nor did he have a mobile phone, so whoever it was could not have tracked him to Devon. He wondered whether to call the police.

No, on second thoughts, that would not be such a good idea. He recalled the warning, delivered barely twenty-four hours earlier by Chris Lopata: "Never trust a copper. They'll shop you as soon as look at you." Why had he said that? He wasn't black and Guy had done nothing wrong. He had once been stopped and questioned by the police after taking a photograph of the Bank of England but that was just the fuzz throwing their weight about. Protecting the national interest, they claimed. Since then, he had lived a charmed life, free from any sort of hassle, apart from bust-ups with a couple of women who had wanted to marry him. Guy valued his freedom and had told them so. He was not going to sacrifice his liberty for the sake of unlimited access to a part of the body that was widely available for hire.

He opened the two letters that had arrived while he was away. One was from the insurance company. Surprise, surprise! The premium for covering his few meagre possessions was going up. He would have been astonished had they told him it was going down. The other was a brief, hand-written note with no address.

Dear Guy [it began], *Please forgive the familiarity but I suspect that we may be on the same wavelength, at least as far as your latest book is concerned. Perhaps we could meet to discuss it some time?*

Yours truly, Max Schulman

Schulman: a Jewish name. Well, that figured. The Jews had done very well out of the Holocaust, screwing billions out of Germany in reparations. They piled on the agony, upping the ante with every new tale of Nazi atrocity to emerge from the history books. They read everything they could get their hands on – except, of course, the UN reports that condemned their illegal occupation of Palestine. They had even tried to recover works of art handed over to the Nazis, albeit under duress, in exchange for their freedom. Now they wanted to renege on the deal, demanding the return of 'their' property while retaining the 'right' to live on land seized from the Arabs. Meanwhile, the world stood by and let them get away with it.

Guy shuffled aimlessly around the room, wondering what to do. Should he call the police? No, that would not solve anything. They'd take one look, ask what was missing, then go away, telling him not to waste their time. What about his neighbours? One of them was a dyed-in-the-wool curtain twitcher, a fully-paid-up member of the Stasi, as far as he could make out. Had they seen anything? They probably wouldn't tell him if they had. He would not demean himself by asking. He decided to sit tight.

He was nevertheless perplexed. Something about Max Schulman's letter, not just the lack of an address, did not ring true. The book had only been out for a few days and not many people would have had a chance to read it. Had Mr Schulman somehow managed to obtain an advance copy? Was he on the publisher's mailing list – a literary critic, perhaps, or possibly even a sales rep? A printer, maybe? They usually knew what was in the pipeline. Indeed, Guy had often wondered how publishers managed to keep a really hot book out of the news until publication day. Some stringent security measures, backed by threats of legal action, must have been employed to prevent the hacks getting hold of a copy.

Suddenly, he thought of the telephone. That might provide a clue as to how his unwanted visitors – if, indeed, there had been any – knew he was not at home. He lifted the receiver to check if anybody had phoned while he was away. Sure enough, two calls on the day he had left for Devonshire. Numbers withheld, no messages. A journalist seeking a few words to fill a column? A sales rep., maybe, but as he was ex-directory that seemed unlikely. As he mulled over the situation, the telephone rang. Was somebody casing the joint – or had he stumbled into the world of the paranormal?

"Hullo," he said, lifting the receiver and trying not to sound rattled. "Guy Chandler."

"Hullo, Guy." The voice was that of a gentleman, cultured and probably quite elderly. "My name is Schulman. I'm sorry to bother you but did you get my letter?"

"I did indeed," said Guy politely.

"Forgive my haste," the caller went on, "but I read the reviews of your book and just had to buy a copy. I find it hard to believe it's just a work of fiction."

"I can assure you it is," said Guy.

"Such a vivid account of the plunder engaged in by the Nazis. One might almost think you were privy to inside information."

"Alas, no."

"Perhaps you're psychic?"

"I'm not Mystic Meg, if that's what you mean."

"A pity! I was going to ask you to read my stars."

"You'd be better off with a fortune teller at the end of the pier," said Guy. "But why the rush, Mr Schulman? You're not an art dealer, by any chance?"

"Let's say I have a professional interest," the caller replied. "I try to keep abreast of all developments in the world of art."

"Even fictional ones?"

"Even fictional ones. That's why I found your book so fascinating and so near the truth."

"Fiction is often stranger than truth," said Guy.

"Disturbingly so, in some respects," Schulman said. "That's really what I wanted to talk to you about. Why don't we meet and have a quiet chat over coffee or something? I may be able to help if you were planning a sequel."

"Well, I hadn't thought of writing another book just yet, not on the same theme, anyway. There's a limited appetite for thrillers about missing pictures."

"I wouldn't be too sure about that," said Schulman. "People always like a good mystery, especially one that involves the Gestapo."

They arranged to meet the following morning at one of the stylish new coffee houses in the City. Guy arrived early and took a seat at one of the small tables. In days gone by, this was how merchants conducted their business, negotiating deals face-to-face over tea or coffee. How much more civilised than the current fad for relying on an algorithm and slinking off to the boys' room for a quick snort when the figures didn't add up.

He recognised Schulman the moment he walked through the door. He was an elderly man of medium height, quite distinguished in a fossilized way, with grey hair and a small moustache. He wore a dark suit, of good quality but less than fashionable, and carried a small briefcase. Nobody would have mistaken him for other than what he appeared to be: a wealthy Jew, possibly from eastern Europe.

"I'm sorry to have kept you waiting," he said, taking a seat. "This is my treat, by the way."

"If you insist," said Guy. Having glanced at the menu, he was not going to pick a fight over 'the reckoning'.

"So," observed his host when the waiter had taken their order, "it's not every day I'm privileged to take coffee with a famous author."

"It's not every day I'm invited to discuss my work with a professional in the world of art," Guy replied.

"I'm sure we'll have a lot to talk about," said Schulman. "Tell me, where did you get your information about the lost Corelli?"

"I made it up," said Guy. "The product of an overstretched imagination."

Mr Schulman smiled and gently stroked one side of his moustache. His well-manicured nails suggested he had not spent much time down a coal mine or on a building site.

"I wish I had an imagination like yours," he said. "You realise that you have painted a remarkably accurate picture of a long-lost masterpiece?"

"A real one?" Guy asked incredulously.

"All too real. And one that my family would dearly like to recover."

"Recover?"

"The *Girl with terracotta pot* – let's not quibble over the title – is a family heirloom – or would have been had it not been stolen by the Gestapo."

"I'm afraid there must be some misunderstanding," said Guy, more than a little bewildered. "As I have already told you, the *The Cartesian triangle* is pure fiction. There's not a word of truth in it."

"Or so the author claims," his host replied. He paused while the waiter set out two cups and poured the coffee. "Really, Guy, am I supposed to believe that you know nothing about a painting that has been missing for 70 years – until it suddenly turns up in a book about the Holocaust?"

Guy was taken aback. "You surely don't think I stole it – the real one, I mean?" he said.

"Of course not. But, according to your fictional account, the painting was discovered during the restoration of an old farmhouse near Grenoble. It just so happens that the Gestapo officer suspected of stealing the picture went to ground in the Chartreuse region after the war. Are you sure, Guy, that you simply made it all up?"

Guy began to wonder if he was losing his mind. He was not an artist and, he was ashamed to admit, had never set foot in the National Gallery. How could he have dreamt up a masterpiece and turned it into his own creation, if only in words? Clearly not by osmosis. The painting of his imagination was conceived solely to provide the plot for a novel which he hoped might earn a few quid. The book was beginning to acquire a Kafkaesque quality.

"I can assure you, Mr..."

"Please call me Max," said Schulman.

"I can assure you, Max, I had no idea I was portraying a real picture. I had done a bit of research, of course, but nothing serious. It must be just one of those fantastic coincidences."

"I am not a great believer in coincidences," said Max.

They fell silent for a moment or two. Schulman played with a forkful of cheesecake, apparently deep in thought. Guy was reminded of those worthy citizens who smiled benignly from the walls of boardrooms across the City. A rogues' gallery, no less. Was Max really a member of the family that had once owned the picture or merely another charlatan? Even if he were a conman, what possible benefit could he derive from a painting that existed only within the pages of a novel? Guy belatedly remembered his training as a journalist.

"I hope you won't be offended, Max," he said, "but would you mind if I asked you to provide some proof of your identity?"

"Not at all," said Schulman. "I'd be most offended if you didn't."

He opened his briefcase and took out a blue folder. Inside were a number of well-worn, almost tatty, photographs. He selected one, of a dignified old man, surrounded by his family in the grounds of a large house, somewhere in Europe. If the clothes worn by the ladies were anything to go by, the family aspired to the haut monde.

"This is my grandfather. The photo was taken in Vienna just before the Anschluss. It was the last anybody ever saw of him. Or of the girl with the terracotta jar."

"What happened to all the other people in the photograph?"

"Most of them perished," said Max, and for the first time Guy thought he detected a trace of a foreign accent.

"Auschwicz?"

"There, and other places."

Guy decided not to pursue the matter. The Holocaust was still too painful for many Jews, although it was clear that Max must have been born after the war.

"Where do you fit in?" he asked.

"My parents were out of the country when war broke out. They survived, along with a handful of others, but nearly all the Viennese clan were wiped out."

"I suppose that when the war ended, the survivors had to start all over again? Or did they still have access to the family fortune?"

"That," said Max, "is a matter of contention."

Guy had no wish to be drawn into a family feud. That was for lawyers to sort out and they would no doubt grow rich in the process.

"I don't suppose you've got a photo of the girl with the pot?" he asked. "Just so that I know what we're talking about."

"I'm afraid not," said Max. "As far as I'm aware, nobody ever captured the painting on film. Life would be a lot easier if they had."

"Can you describe it?"

"Certainly. It shows a young lady, East African, I'd guess, standing next to a large pot made of clay. Colourful clothes, plenty of sunshine. A touch of Polynesia about it, even though it's clearly set in Africa."

"That's exactly how I imagined it," said Guy. "Perhaps I *am* psychic."

"Or just have a good memory."

Guy had heard of authors who, by sheer accident, had managed to write stories that proved remarkably prescient. He recalled one such tale that more or less predicted the death of a famous comedian while on tour in Australia. The author was flabbergasted and struggled to explain how an entirely fictional account had, within eighteen months, turned out to be true. Guy was beginning to suspect that *The Cartesian triangle* came into the same category. However, he perceived a small gap in Schulman's story.

"Tell me, Max," he said. "If you have never seen this painting, how are you able to describe it?"

For a moment, Schulman appeared nonplussed. He stared briefly at the photo while gathering his wits.

"Because for years the family could speak of nothing else," he said, forcing a smile. "The painting has been absorbed into our genetic code."

"Is it very valuable?"

"That depends on how you define value," said Max, now fully recovered. "It's unlikely to be snapped up as an investment by a Japanese bank – or even an Austrian one, come to that. But money's not everything."

"It is for most collectors."

"In this case, other factors are involved."

"Such as?"

"Family history. The painting was acquired from the artist by my grandfather. He may even have commissioned it; I'm not sure."

"Seems an odd subject for a commission. Most are for portraits."

"Don't forget that Germany once owned a chunk of East Africa," said Max. "My grandfather went there as a young man. He spent several years in the bush, setting up trading posts in various places. The painting may have told some story or other."

"Of an illicit liaison with a lady of colour?" Guy suggested.

"Could be," Max agreed. "The desire for – how do you say, a bit of fluff - seldom takes the colour of skin into account."

"True," said Guy, who had cast many a lustful glance at the products of diversity as he travelled about London.

"Whatever it was, the secret died with my grandfather."

"Or fell into the hands of the Gestapo?"

"Quite," said Max.

The waiter, one of those foreigners who polluted the Tube with their strange accents every morning, arrived with a fresh pot of coffee. In another century, the scene might have been that of a café in Vienna. The smell of coffee, the delicious pastries, the well-heeled clientele. All that was missing was a gypsy fiddler.

"More coffee, sir?" the waiter asked.

"Yes, please," said Guy. "The best coffee I've tasted for a long time."

"Thank you, sir."

Max waited for his own cup to be refilled and then said: "Corelli always reminds me of Gauguin. Similar style, same use of colour. Vivid splashes, exotic backgrounds. Did you study art, by the way?"

"No. I'm a writer. I just thought the discovery of a painting assumed to have been lost would make a good story, that's all."

"It certainly does."

Max finished his cheesecake and said: "Gauguin was a stockbroker, you know. On the Paris bourse. He chucked it all to become a painter."

"I didn't know, but he'd probably have made more money by sticking to shares."

"Not if he had the sort of shares I've got!" quipped Max. "He was older than Corelli, of course, but they clearly belong to the same school. I must remember to enrol you one day."

"I'd be more than honoured," said Guy. "It's a pity I can't paint,"

"Except with words," said Max. "And there, if I may say so, you are a true artist."

He wiped his moustache and put the photos back in his briefcase. "By the way," he added, extracting a copy of *The Cartesian triangle*, "I wonder if you'd be kind enough to sign your book for me? Just to show that I've met the author."

"With pleasure," said Guy.

Taking his fountain pen (young fogeys did not use Biros) from his inner pocket, he carefully inscribed a few words on the title page.

"Thank you," said Max. "I shall treasure the book even more now."

He smiled and, taking two crisp £10 notes from his wallet, left them by the side of his plate to settle the bill.

"We must stay in touch," he added as they prepared to leave. "I'm sure that when you've had time to think, you'll appreciate that you must have seen this picture somewhere. I would dearly love to know where."

They said goodbye. As he watched his companion depart, Guy realised he still didn't know where Max Schulman lived. Nor had he been given any proof of his identity. He had, however, provided a perfect specimen of his own signature.

Chapter V

Guy never tired of exploring the City, or what was left of it. The financial capital, although still home to the Bank of England, was beginning to show its age. Its nose had been put right out of joint by the brash upstart to the east, which even had its own railway and airport, ironically called the City airport. Guy could never understand why the Corporation had allowed the Docklands to develop. The project should have been strangled at birth, before it could lure skills and talent away from the historic centre of power. Now, when the Isle of Dogs barked, the aldermen of the City of London simply threw it another bone.

The Square Mile nevertheless still vibrated with pageantry and tradition. The Lord Mayor's show, the ravens and beefeaters of the Tower of London, even the swans on the River Thames, all conspired to evoke the glories of the past. Despite the cranes and the scaffolding, history oozed from every corbel and cornerstone. Statues of men who helped to lay the foundations of Empire abounded. Guy was proud of their contribution to history – and to the wealth of the nation. Without them, the City would probably have withered on the vine. Across the river, people still flocked to the Globe where the plays attributed to Shakespeare were first produced.

The City was not just about trade and the Bard, however. One or two people still actually lived there. Not as many as worked there, of course, but enough to provide some semblance of life after the markets had closed. Some of the newer residents were giving the place a bad name, however. Russian hitmen, Nigerian conmen, fraudsters of every nationality. Was Max Schulman one of them? Guy had meant to ask how his parents had escaped from Europe and when they had arrived in Britain – if, indeed, they had. Were the Schulmans now British subjects and, if so, where had Max gone to school? His accent revealed no trace of a foreign upbringing, apart from the one tantalising hint when they were discussing the fate of the Viennese branch of the family. Like Miss Kovalski, he might almost have been British.

He walked up Lombard Street, wondering how much longer the few remaining older structures would be able to hold out against speculators and developers. The Nazis preferred portable property but greed and corruption were the same in any language. It was far more profitable to tear down an historic building than plunder a museum packed with works of art. The stolen artefacts could never be sold openly on the market; new buildings were simply off-loaded to the highest bidder. In recent years, much of the money used to prop up the property market had come from Russia. The once-impoverished citizens of the Soviet Union now owned thousands of houses across London and the Home Counties. The City, especially, had become one giant Laundromat for handling dirty money stolen from the state. The British government seemed strangely reluctant to name and shame the thieves.

Guy was about to cross the road when he stopped to let a car pass. The vehicle was unmarked but it was clearly a police car. Two coppers in uniform, looking smug and self-satisfied, as well they might on fifty grand a year, sat in front. On the back seat, a woman in a denim jacket was talking on the phone. The driver was in no hurry and Guy had a chance to observe her. He caught his breath. Unless he was mistaken, the passenger was none other than Miss Kovalski. She was engrossed in conversation and obviously hadn't seen him. Her jacket was open, revealing a blouse of many colours, and even her hair was vaguely psychedelic; in fact, he thought he detected a turquoise streak. She was certainly not the well-groomed young woman he had seen only a few weeks ago. More like a hippy, he thought. But, then, she was the arty type, wasn't she? Dartington College, he recalled. How else did he expect her to look?

Guy wondered whether his imagination was running away with him. He knew the mind played tricks when an obsession took hold. That's how ghosts came into being. If it was her, was she under arrest or just touring the City, helping the fuzz to identify a suspect? For a few seconds, the obvious answer eluded him. The Lopatas had told him she had joined the police but he had been strangely reluctant to believe them. Now here was the evidence, *prima facie* but nevertheless compelling. She was a copper, in all probability one of the plain-clothes variety. The blue denim suggested she was not rostered for point-duty outside Buckingham Palace. The car drove on. Guy was left standing on the pavement, dumbfounded.

He resisted the temptation to have a stiff drink and instead took the Tube to Fulham. He needed to consult Robert, his publicist. He would know what to do. It was at times like this that Guy wished he had more friends. But writers were solitary creatures and had to confront most crises on their own. A few comforting words from a business colleague was the most he could expect. The fare did nothing to improve his temper. How could people afford to travel by public transport in London these days? The train drivers were holding the public over a barrel with their never-ending demands. Nothing less than daylight robbery. The sooner robots took over, the better. By the time he reached Fulham Broadway, he was in a bolshie frame of mind. A notice inviting him to 'Alight here for the National Hospital for Nervous Diseases' did nothing to calm his nerves. At this rate, he would soon need an appointment with the shrink himself. He hurried to his agent's office.

"I've found her," he gasped.

"Found who?" enquired Robert.

"Miss Smith."

"I thought her name was Kazinski?"

"Kovalski," Guy corrected him. "In the back of a police car."

"So, what do you want me to do? Stand bail?"

"But, don't you see?" Guy implored. "She must be one of them."

Robert studied the author for a second or two, then drew a deep breath.

"For a journalist, you are somewhat over-inclined to jump to conclusions," he said. "Just because you see a woman in a black Maria..."

"Police car..."

". . you think she must be a rozzer. She might have been a shoplifter. Or even a human resources consultant. How can you be sure it was her, anyway?"

"Because . . I've been thinking about her more or less every day since we first met. Her face is imprinted on my memory."

"Hallucinations," said Robert. "Happens to all middle-aged gentlemen smitten by some floozie."

"She's not a floozie," Guy said protectively. "But why didn't she tell me she was a police officer?"

"If I were a copper, I wouldn't shout about it. It's not something to be proud of, exactly. Anyway, perhaps you didn't ask."

"That's true. I didn't. But it still doesn't explain why she turned up at the launch."

"Maybe she's just a nice Jewish girl who's interested in the Holocaust."

"That's conceivable," said Guy.

"Well, if you do find her, just make sure that Miss Kovalski isn't."

Sympathy was clearly in short supply this morning. Hopefully, it was only because the agent saw no mileage in the heart-ache of one of his clients.

"Tell me, Robert," said Guy. "Do you think there's anything in the book that could provoke a backlash?"

"For Christ's sake! You're the bloody author! Don't you know what you wrote about?"

"Sure I do. But look what happened to Rushdie. I don't want to be like him, having to be protected all the time."

"I'd have thought that if it meant Miss Kazinski holding your hand all day you'd welcome it. But remember this: Britain is a Christian country, not some feudal Islamic state, like Iran or Pakistan. Our right to say what we think is underwritten by law."

"Until you try to say it," Guy reminded him.

"You're not going to be brow-beaten by a bunch of snowflakes, are you?"

"No, but I don't want to end up dead, either."

"Try to look on the positive side," said Robert. "Just think of all the publicity we could screw out of a death threat."

"You're not on the receiving end."

"Neither are you, so stop wasting my time – and try not to get bundled into the back of a paddy wagon."

"That," said Guy, "is a politically-incorrect term that the Irish might find offensive."

"Stuff the Irish," said Robert. "You'll be telling me next that Taffy's not a Welshman. Now, I must bid you good-day. I have work to do."

Like the ploughman at the end of a hard day among the organic cabbages, Guy plodded his weary way homewards to Blackheath. The Stasi were waiting for him in the foyer.

"Hi, Guy," said the not-so-secret policeman, fiddling with a bit of rag he was using to clean the door handle of his own flat. "How's it going?"

"Fine, thanks," said Guy, fishing out his key. He wondered how long this obnoxious individual had been hanging about, waiting to question him. The door handle must be the cleanest in Blackheath.

"I've been reading about you in the papers," the snoop said. "You seem to have made quite a splash with your new book."

"A few ripples, that's all," said Guy, opening the door. "They'll soon be ironed out by the tide."

"There is a tide in the affairs of men . ." the twitcher declaimed proudly. "I wish I could write."

"What's stopping you?"

"No time," the aspiring author said. "By the way," he added, clearly more anxious to discuss the affairs of men than his ability to string a few words together, "you had a visitor the other day."

"Yes, I know," said Guy, dissembling with a fluency that startled him. "A friend of mine."

"I didn't know you had any lady friends. I'd always thought you must be . ."

"Some kind of poofter? Sorry to disappoint you."

Guy stepped inside and closed the door. So, his mysterious visitor was a woman, was she? Well, that didn't surprise him. What sort of man would wear a scent that lingered for more than 24 hours? Somebody who thought deodorant was a substitute for soap and water, maybe.

Only one woman sprang to mind: the female plod with the denim jacket and turquoise hair. Copper she might be but nobody let themselves into his flat without permission – and certainly not with a skeleton key or a bit of wire. He was not going to put up with that. Some explanation was needed.

With mounting anger, he flipped through the phone book, searching for the City of London police. He found the number and dialled.

"Could I speak to Miss Kovalski, please?" he said when his call was answered.

"One moment, sir." A short pause. "How are you spelling that?"

Guy spelled out the name, or how he thought she might spell it.

"I'm sorry, sir. We don't appear to have anybody of that name. Are you sure she works for the City of London police?"

Guy wasn't sure. There were dozens of police forces across Britain, even one for Devon and Cornwall. Not forgetting Thames Valley and the Met., of course. He couldn't phone them all; it would cost a fortune and he'd lose patience after the first half dozen. He rang off.

He was both irritated and hungry. He opened the fridge only to find that, like Old Mother Hubbard's cupboard, it was distressingly bare. Thanks to his rendezvous with Schulman, he had forgotten to buy any food. Stuffing a plastic bag into his pocket, he headed for Tesco.

At least the Stasi had given up waiting in the foyer.

Chapter VI

If the days before publication made him anxious and twitchy, the month that followed was usually marked by post-natal depression and lethargy. This time, however, Guy was more than a little restless. Like most authors, he could not survive on the income from his books alone. Now that he had given up his day job as a reporter, he needed something to keep him occupied – and reasonably well-nourished – until his next royalty cheque arrived. He was lucky in that he knew somebody at Crosbie, Grimshaw and Snape, a small advertising agency that often relied on freelance writers. Creative people were always in demand, as was clear from the inflated salaries offered to anyone with a modicum of wit. He decided to give them a ring.

"We could use somebody at the moment," the creative director said. "A spot of copy writing, if you're interested."

"Tell me more," said Guy. "I like to eat."

"I'd have thought that a renowned author like yourself could afford to eat at least twice a day," the adman responded.

"Irony is still in vogue, I see."

"Why not drop in and we'll have a chat?"

Next morning, Guy made his way to the smart, stylish offices of CGS in the West End. The ambience was elegant and sophisticated, far removed from the traditional milieu of the Guildhall. This was the place where dreams of a perfect skin or new washing machine were manufactured to keep advertisers happy and consumers in thrall. Even the furniture -- designed to impress clients rather than comfort aching joints -- emitted an air of unreality. Guy wondered how much extra he was paying for his cornflakes and razor blades to finance such pretensions. After a brief chat with the creative director, he agreed to start work the following Monday.

Guy was not over-enthusiastic about sitting at a desk all day but nevertheless enjoyed striving to find a catchy phrase that might persuade people to buy some product or other. It was an intellectual challenge, constrained only by the demand that ads. be legal, decent and honest. The era of snake-oil salesmen had long since passed. And, he tried to convince himself, there was nothing demeaning about writing advertising copy. After all, one of the 20th Century's most famous ads. – My Goodness! My Guinness! – had been penned by none other than Dorothy L. Sayers, creator of Lord Peter Wimsey. Guy wished that he, too, could scribble something that would go down in advertising history, preferably before he himself was struck down by pre-senile dementia.

Another writer, also a woman, had come up with the slogan 'Go to work on an egg'. That was before people started worrying about their cholesterol, of course, a distinctly unhealthy obsession that had knocked the bottom out of the egg market. That, and salmonella. And what about 'Time for a tiger', a few words eagerly anticipated by beer drinkers at the end of a long, hot and steamy day in the Far East? Anthony Burgess had appropriated them for the title of one of his novels – and if anyone knew about beer in the Far East it was Anthony Burgess.

Guy figured the job would do more than put a few pennies into his bank account. It would help take his mind off Miss Kovalski as well as provide an opportunity to discuss paintings with Grant, the agency's art supremo. Unlike Guy, he had studied art at college.

"Corelli?" he mused when Guy found an excuse to drop in to his studio. "A fairly mediocre talent, in my opinion. Not in the first rank, by any means, and certainly not in the same class as Hogarth or Constable. He did occasionally produce some good work, however. Why do you ask?"

Guy repeated the story of how the girl with the earthenware jar had taken over his life.

"Incredible," said Grant. "I don't believe it."

"Improbable, I know," said Guy. "But that's how it is."

"Are you sure you hadn't seen the picture years ago when you were wandering around Europe as a penniless student?"

"How could I have seen it, when the real painting was stolen by the Gestapo long before I was born?"

"That doesn't mean it hasn't resurfaced. Pictures looted by the

Nazis are turning up all the time."

"Not in my neck of the woods."

"There was a whole cache discovered just the other day, in Austria or some such place," Grant reminded him. "The guy who owned the apartment had been sitting on them for more than half a century."

"I hope he's got a good lawyer."

"He clearly didn't have many visitors. None who showed much curiosity, anyway. What about a photo?"

"I'm told there isn't one."

"Then you must have read about it somewhere. That's how the creative process often works. Ideas lie dormant for years, like seeds in an old pasture. Then along comes the ploughman and – hey, presto! – they spring to life. Your girl with the crock of gold has been lying fallow, waiting to sprout, since the day you first saw her, whenever that was."

"You don't think there's something about the painting that points to a crock of gold?" asked Guy.

"Is there a rainbow in the background?"

"Not in my version."

"Then there isn't any gold, either."

Grant carefully arranged the pencils and felt-tipped pens on his desk, an infallible sign to his colleagues in the agency that he was about to deliver a judgement.

"The problem with paintings that suddenly turn up after being lost for years," he said, "is that they often turn out to be fakes. Remember the Hitler diaries? Complete fabrication."

"How could a work of fiction be other than fabricated?" asked Guy.

"I'm not talking about your book; I'm talking about the girl with the terracotta pot, claimed by your friend, Mr Schulman."

"You don't think he's a conman, do you, trying to get his hands on a painting that might be worth a bob or two?"

"I don't know what to think," said Grant. "The whole business is quite absurd. Surreal, even."

"I agree. If it goes on like this, I'll have to be put away."

"At least you'll be in good company. Hemingway, Virginia Woolf, John Clare – they all had to be locked up at some stage. Poor Clare for the rest of his life."

"Great wits to madness are near allied," quoth Guy,

and thin partitions do their bounds divide..."

"Dryden," said Grant. "Although anybody who regards Virginia Woolf as witty deserves to be locked up. What account are you working on, by the way?"

"The new, environment-friendly weedkiller," said Guy. "The one that singles out wild oats but spares seagulls."

"That'll drive you round the bend, all right. After grappling with the Wildlife and Countryside Act for a few days, you'll wish you were back with the girl with the crock of gold."

"Earthenware jar," said Guy.

He returned to his desk and began to compose an ad. that didn't breach the law or offend the fur and feather brigade. His task was to promote a weedkiller that did not harm wildlife, even though it deprived them of their habitat and source of food. He felt like a barrister called upon to defend a villain on the grounds that to put him away might breach his human rights. Guy was all in favour of human rights, particularly those that gave humans the right to shoot seagulls and other scavengers. As far as he was concerned, they belonged to the same family as badgers; a protected species that did little more than spread disease. By the end of the day, he'd had enough of weeds and herring gulls and vowed never to vote Green again. He might even lobby his MP to repeal the Act that allowed these filthy birds to wreak havoc wherever they went. But at least his efforts would put some money into his bank account.

He was heading across town towards Charing Cross, hoping not to attract the attention of the pigeons in Trafalgar Square, when a paper boy thrust a wad of newsprint into his hand. Guy was far too young to remember the days when London had three evening papers, the Star, News and Standard. The Star had been the first to go, followed many years later by the News. Now only the Standard remained and that had to be given away to ensure advertisers got value for money. Television was no longer the main threat; even it was being hammered by social media which soaked up marketing budgets. Yet people still read newspapers which they thought could be relied on for accuracy, poor fools.

The train was crowded, forcing him to stand all the way to Blackheath, so he tucked the paper under his arm and waited until he got home before reading it. There was no sign of the Stasi although he thought he saw a curtain quiver. That probably meant no visitors; otherwise, the grubby little tyke would have been there, in the foyer, bursting to tell him. He let himself in and put the kettle on. Finding a slice of quiche, he popped it in the oven to warm up, then made a pot of tea and slumped on the sofa. It had been a tiring, although exhilarating, day. He opened the paper. Brexit, Brexit, Brexit. He was sick to death of stories about MPs trying to thwart the will of the people. The sooner these shysters got their comeuppance and Britain left the EU, the better. A small news item on Page 17 caught his eye.

Man dies after random shooting

> An elderly man wounded in what appears to have been a random shooting two days ago has died in hospital. He never regained consciousness after being gunned down in a London street. Police are appealing for help to identify him. He is described as white, of medium build, with a small moustache. Apart from banknotes -- some of which, say police, have proved to be counterfeit -- his wallet contained only a telephone number. Anyone with information should contact Scotland Yard.

Guy's blood ran cold. The description -- an Identikit picture in words -- fitted Max like a glove. He was still reeling from shock and trying to grasp the enormity of the story when the telephone rang. He put down the paper and went into the hall to answer it.

"Good evening, sir," said a voice. "I'm sorry to bother you but I am Detective Sergeant Matthews of Scotland Yard . . "

"Don't tell me," said Guy, dreading what the copper might say. "I've just read about it."

"Read about what, sir?"

"The old boy in hospital. That's why you're phoning, isn't it?"

"Did you know the gentleman, sir?"

"If it's who I think it is, I can only say I met him for the first time a few days ago. We had coffee together."

"Can you remember his name?"

"Max Schulman. At least, that's what he called himself."

"Had you any reason to think it was not his real name?"

"None at all. All I know is that his family came from Vienna. I guess there must be a lot of Schulmans in that part of the world."

Guy realised he was being drawn into a mystery that was, he had to admit, partly of his own making. If only he hadn't written about the girl with the earthenware potty or agreed to meet Max Schulman for coffee!

"If you barely knew him, sir, I wonder how your telephone number came to be in his wallet?"

"My telephone number?"

Guy suddenly felt very faint. His eyes refused to focus and the room gave a tentative spin. Not another attack of vertigo, he hoped. The last one caused him to black out. He leant against the wall and tried to marshal his thoughts.

"Are you all right, sir?" asked the man at the Met.

"A little dizzy, that's all," said Guy. "It's not every day that somebody you know is shot dead in the street."

"I quite understand, sir. The news must have come as a bit of a shock."

"You could say that."

"I don't want to add to your distress, sir, but I wonder if we could pop round and have a word with you? We need to identify this gentleman as soon as possible."

"You know where I live, I guess?"

"We'll find you."

Detective Sergeant Matthews and a colleague arrived within the hour. They parked their car and rang the bell. Guy was relieved they were not in uniform but wondered if the twitcher had noted their arrival. He invited them in and explained the circumstances of his meeting with Max Schulman. He showed them the letter he had received. The sergeant read it and asked if he could take it away.

"It may be needed as evidence," he said.

"Evidence of what?" asked Guy.

"Murder. Mr Schulman obviously didn't shoot himself."

"But why should anyone want to kill him?"

"That's what we were hoping you might be able to tell us, sir."

"You're not implying that it was I who shot him?" Guy retorted, stung by the suggestion that he might have murdered somebody.

"Of course not, sir. But we are investigating a crime. We like to keep an open mind."

"Have you checked the spy cameras? Aren't they supposed to prevent and detect crime?"

"Unfortunately," said Matthews, "there were no security cameras in this particular street. It's one of the few in London not subject to surveillance."

"Whoever killed him must have known that."

"Possibly."

"Do you own a gun, sir?" asked the other copper, a hard-faced man with a belligerent look.

"No, but I'm told they're fairly easy to acquire in London these days."

"I was only asking, sir."

Never trust a copper, Chris Lopata had said. Given half a chance, they'll stitch you up. Guy decided that a pre-emptive strike was the best form of defence.

"If I wanted to kill somebody," he said, "I wouldn't shoot them. Too noisy – and it's difficult to remove the traces of gunpowder."

"How would you go about it then, sir?"

"I'd probably use poison. That's the fashionable way, I believe. Anthrax – or polonium, maybe. Just a speck in their tea, or coffee. The Russians could probably tell me how to do it."

The two coppers exchanged glances. Were they being sent up or was this guy a complete nutter, capable of wiping out half of London with a phial of Novichok?

"You seem to be well-informed, sir. Have you ever thought of killing anybody?"

"Often," said Guy. "But they've always won a last-minute reprieve. I still harbour murderous thoughts towards seagulls, though."

After a moment or two's thought, the sergeant decided that Guy was apparently harmless, if a trifle eccentric.

"Mr Schulman appeared to be quite wealthy, sir," he continued. "Yet his wallet contained several banknotes that proved to be counterfeit. Would you care to hazard a guess as to how they came to be there?"

"I've no idea," said Guy. "Perhaps he printed them -- although the new tenners . . "

He paused, recalling the two crisp £10 notes that Max had produced to pay the bill.

"What about them, sir?"

"I was going to say the new tenners are supposed to be fake-proof. It's only the old paper-based twenties that can be passed off with any degree of confidence."

The cops said nothing but looked at him in a strange way. Guy could understand why people being interrogated often said things they didn't mean. In the hands of a copper trying to nail a suspect, their words could easily be taken out of context and presented as an admission of guilt. The fuzz were not beyond writing out confessions, either, which somebody under pressure would sign, even if they were innocent. He was determined not to be intimidated.

"Perhaps you would be kind enough to answer one or two of my questions?" he said.

"If we can, sir."

"Max Schulman. Was that his real name?"

"We know only as much as you do, sir," the sergeant said, glancing at the letter now in his possession. "Unless you know something you haven't told us about."

"I'm beginning to think I know nothing about him at all," said Guy. "In fact, I'm beginning to wish I'd never written the damned book."

"What book is that, sir?"

Guy slumped on the couch and ran his fingers through his hair. *The Cartesian triangl*e was driving him mad. A sudden flash of inspiration made him say: "Why not ask Miss Kovalski?"

"Miss Kovalski?" said Matthews. "Who's she?"

"I thought you might be able to tell me," Guy said pointedly.

The two police officers exchanged a further meaningful glance. Good cop, bad cop. There were no prizes for guessing who was which. Bad cop took it upon himself to answer.

"I don't know anybody of that name, sir, not at the Yard, anyway. Is she a friend of yours?"

"I've only met her once, and that was very briefly. I thought perhaps she might be one of your mob."

"A police officer, you mean?"

"If that's how you'd like to describe her."

"I wouldn't like to describe anybody I didn't know."

Sergeant Matthews decided they were not going to get much more out of this touchy suburban scribbler. It was time for some mandatory cooperation.

"There's one other matter on which we would appreciate your help, sir," he said. "As you're the only person to have met the deceased, I'm afraid we must ask you to accompany us to the morgue to identify him."

"When, now?" asked Guy.

"If it's not inconvenient, sir."

"Okay. If we must. We might as well get it over and done with."

"Thank you, sir. It's only a formality. We will, of course, drive you there and back."

"Do you drive, sir?" asked Bellicose Bill.

"I have a licence, if that's what you mean."

"You don't own a car?"

"No. I'm an author, not a company rep."

Guy swallowed a mouthful of cold tea, then realised the quiche was still in the oven. He rushed to recover it, only to find a crisp, uneatable slice of pastry. He wondered whether to invoice Scotland Yard. *Victuals, to wit, one slice of quiche, ruined in pursuit of justice, £1.*

With Bellicose Bill at the wheel of the unmarked vehicle, they drove swiftly through the evening traffic, heading north and crossing the river. Guy sat in the back. Was there, perhaps, an equally simple explanation for Miss Kovalski's presence in the back of a police car? Maybe he had been too quick to draw conclusions, as his agent had suggested.

Within a few minutes, they arrived at the hospital where Max had died.

"Have you ever seen a dead body, sir?" asked Sergeant Matthews as the porter, in green hospital garb, escorted them to the morgue.

"No. That's one pleasure that's been denied me," said Guy.

"It can be quite gruesome but fortunately Mr Schulman died from a single bullet wound. He's been cleaned up, anyway. It won't take long."

The porter unlocked the door and directed them towards a table on which the body lay. He pulled back the sheet covering the face and Sergeant Matthews invited Guy to step forward.

"Take your time, sir. Your information is crucial."

Guy stared at the immobile features of the man who not long

ago had been so full of life. The skin was sallow and the eyes closed. The moustache was still neatly trimmed although some stubble had appeared on the chin. He resisted the temptation to have one last look at those well-manicured nails, now hidden by the sheet, to see whether they had also continued to grow. That this was the body of the man known to him as Max Schulman he had no doubt.

"That's him, all right," he said, turning away and shivering slightly. "Poor old bugger."

"Are you sure, sir?" asked Matthews.

"Absolutely," said Guy.

The porter covered the body and they returned to the car. Guy battled to control his nausea. He was not, he realised, cut out to be a pathologist.

"If you could just drive me to Charing Cross," he said, "I'll take the train. I need some fresh air."

"I know the feeling, sir," the sergeant said, opening the door for him. "If I had a choice, I'd much prefer to identify the living."

They drove down the Strand, packed with early-evening revellers, and pulled into the forecourt of Charing Cross station, ignoring the protests of taxi drivers. Sergeant Matthews got out and extended his hand.

"I'm much obliged for your help, sir," he said. "If we do manage to confirm the gentleman's name, you'll be among the first to know."

"Thank you," said Guy. "I'm not under arrest, then?"

"Not at the moment, sir," said Bellicose Bill.

Chapter VII

Guy was beginning to feel badly in need of a holiday. The Azores again hovered seductively on the horizon. A week or two there, or even in Alicante, would take his mind off the vicissitudes of life in London. The problem, as usual, was money. He could not really afford to stop work, just to lie in the sun or linger over a meal in some trendy eating house. He had already wasted enough time chasing shadows in Newton Abbot. He decided to call his publisher and enquire how sales were going.

"It's not exactly flying off the shelves," the publisher said. "But it's not doing too badly, either."

"I won't be able to retire just yet, then?"

"Not for a while, I'd say. We've had one encouraging sign, however."

"What sort of sign?"

"An order from Zurich. Only for a couple of copies, but we don't sell many books in Switzerland, even at the best of times."

"Perhaps the gnomes have run out of reading matter?"

"Could be. You can't dine out for ever on the latest OECD forecast. If they order any more, I'll let you know."

Guy took the hint. His publisher had other offspring to humour and indulge. He could not spend all day talking to an author whose book was now in the shops and who would get a royalty statement, and possibly a cheque, in due course. Guy thanked him and hung up.

He sat down at his computer and checked his bank account. That, at least, had not been compromised. He was comfortably in the black, thanks to Crosbie, Grimshaw and Snape, and provided he did not go overboard, could afford a week or so at one of the less-fashionable resorts. Somewhere not too far, so that the fare alone would not plunge him into the red. France, maybe. For some reason, Grenoble crossed his mind. He ruled that out immediately. *The Cartesian triangle,* set partly in Grenoble, had already caused more than enough aggro. Besides, it was scarcely a resort; probably expensive, too. He scrolled through the special offers on various websites and opted for Perpignan, not far from the border with Spain. Ten days there would not force him to seek protection from his creditors. The plonk in that part of the world was barely drinkable but he was not obliged to support the region's vineyards.

Early one morning, when he hoped the twitcher would be still in bed or having breakfast, he slunk out of the flat and took the train to Gatwick. From there, it was but a simple journey – no more than two hours by plane – to Perpignan. Once on the ground, he would be driven straight to his hotel. That was the great thing about packaged holidays; initiative was unnecessary. When Laurie Lee walked out that midsummer morning almost a century earlier, he had to do everything for himself, even carry his dinner – a tin of treacle biscuits and a bit of cheese. These days, the travel companies ensured that customers did not even have to think. Designed for plebs, of course, but beggars – and authors – could not be choosers. He prepared for a traumatic few days among the proletariat.

He was glad they were flying from Gatwick. He hated Heathrow, Britain's biggest airport, and did everything he could to avoid it. On one occasion, when travelling to Rome, he had contemplated flying from Bristol but calculated he would spend more time on the M5 than in the departure lounge at Heathrow. Gritting his teeth, he had headed for Terminal One.

Now he was at Gatwick, looking out across the green fields of Surrey. He still had to wait but for once everything seemed to be going smoothly. No drones or stray cattle near the runway to disrupt the schedule. Planes and passengers came and went, children looking forward to their first trip abroad ran around excitedly. He hoped they wouldn't be sick. Years earlier, while crossing the Andes by bus, a horrible child was sick over everything. Sorry, it's the altitude, the mother explained. Guy thought it more likely to be too many sweets, exacerbated by the long journey over the mountains. He was glad that on the aircraft kids would be tied down, at least for some of the time.

"British Airways announces Flight 361 to Geneva," came a voice over the public-address system. "Will passengers please make their way to the departure gate."

How many times had he heard that in various languages? He watched the passengers gather their belongings and shuffle towards the gate, boarding passes in hand. Most appeared to be salesmen; self-important dogsbodies in suits (Guy had forsaken his and was travelling in jeans), thinking more of their expense accounts than their order books. He wagered that none was a publisher's rep. One or two financial consultants, maybe, but nobody planning to climb the Matterhorn or sell a few watches. He felt a twinge of admiration for Max's grandfather who had trekked through the African bush, braving crocodiles and tse-tse flies to negotiate deals with tribal elders.

A woman in the queue attracted his attention. Although her back was towards him, something about her was all too familiar. Well-groomed, nice legs, neat little botty. His heart skipped a beat. Was it her? Who else could it have been? This time her hair was brown. No turquoise streaks or hippy gear. She looked as though she had never worn a denim jacket in her life. What was she doing, en route to Geneva? Not to discuss police matters, that's for sure. Interpol was based in Lyon, not Lausanne. At least she was by herself, which possibly meant that she didn't have a bloke. Or if she did she was heading for the Continent without him.

He wondered whether to chase after her. No, that would only ring alarm bells and bring Security out in force. The last thing he wanted was to spark off an incident and find himself splashed over the front pages. He could do without that kind of publicity. By the time he had decided what to do she had gone through the metal detectors. What business was it of his, anyway, that she was travelling to Switzerland? They had met only once and she had probably forgotten him. Always poking her nose into other people's affairs, Chris Lopata had said. That description might well apply to himself. He lay back and swallowed his disappointment.

Geneva: not far from Zurich. How could it be? Switzerland was a small country, not even a member of the EU. The two cities could not be more than a few miles apart, even as the cuckoo flew. Geneva, on the lake, in the south; Zurich to the north, in the hills. Both rivalled Monte Carlo as the home of shady people and secret bank accounts. Despite its claim to be more transparent nowadays, the country was once again regarded as a safe haven for illicit funds. A lot of Russian money – some of it said to belong to Very Important Persons in the Kremlin – had apparently found its way there. Why would Miss Kovalski be heading for such a destination? Was she hot on the trail of ill-gotten roubles or were the police now paid so much they could afford to bank in Switzerland? He'd heard of one copper who commuted from his home in South Africa when called upon to perform constabulary duties in London. Perhaps she was simply a bookworm and wanted to see where Mary Shelley gave birth to *Frankenstein*.

A relaxing holiday in the foothills of the Pyrenees was now out of the question. He would be thinking about her every day, wondering whether she was still among the clocks and cuckoos or back in London, driving about the City in a paddy wagon. Or black Maria.

His flight was called and he made his way through the departure lounge. The chief steward, lovely and leggy, welcomed him aboard and flashed him a smile that banished Miss Kovalski to the outer reaches of space. She glanced at his seat number and directed him towards the tail. That was the safest part of the aircraft apparently. If it crashed, he would still be in with a chance. He just hoped the person next to him knew the meaning of deodorant. He empathised with cabin crews forced to smile as they catered to the whims of passengers who stank like polecats. He needn't have worried; the seat was unoccupied. He fastened his seatbelt and prepared for take-off.

The plane taxied down the runway and in a few minutes they were airborne. Somewhere below, hidden by clouds, lay the South Downs. Guy soon gave up looking. He was heading for the sun and there was no place his itinerary for grey skies. All those warnings about skin cancer were brushed aside as he contemplated a few hatless days in the south of France, absorbing Vitamin D.

This was a no-frills flight which meant that if he wanted a drink he would have to pay for it. Nor was there any food to assuage the pangs of hunger. He hoped there was a doctor on board to treat those who could not survive for ninety minutes without filling their gut with rubber chicken. Almost before he'd had time to read the brochures stuffed into the seat in front of him, they were circling Perpignan and had begun their descent. The plane touched down and skidded to a halt. He said goodbye to the leggy lovely and collected his luggage. The sun and the Pyrenees beckoned.

He looked around for the coach that was supposed to take him from the airport to the hotel. Plenty of people but no sign of either coach or driver. He needn't have worried. Within half an hour he and other passengers booked into the same hotel had been rounded up and were on their way. Guy eyed them warily; all seemed reasonably couth and civilised. No nasty little habits (at least, none that he could see) that might cast a shadow over his holiday. Perhaps he was being too sniffy. After all, they might be the sort of people who read books and might even buy a copy of *The Cartesian triangle* if he drew their attention to it. For the time being, however, he decided to maintain a fogeyish reserve.

The hotel, just off the main street, was comfortable and well-appointed. No swimming pool, but who wanted a pool when the sea and the mountains were close at hand? Pools were for plebs. The kitchen and dining room were more important, the chef even more so. He looked forward to his first meal. Not cheval bordelaise avec frites gratin, he hoped, or anything wrapped in pastry. He liked to see what he was eating. The staff were polite and efficient, displaying no hint of the patronage often reserved for Brits. The Frogs would do anything for money, Guy reflected, even hide their contempt for the packaged proles who kept them in business. The question was how to spend his time in this quiet corner of France without thinking of the woman who was hundreds of miles away in Geneva – if, indeed, that's where she was. He vowed to make every effort to put her out of his mind.

Perpignan was a small town and, despite the ancient ramparts, he soon tired of wandering the dusty streets. There was only so much history one could digest without resorting to a glass of that undrinkable wine. He decided to take a short trip to Figueras, just over the border in Spain. A fine hill town, ravaged by war, wrote Laurie Lee who spent a few days there during the Spanish civil war. He had trudged over the mountains to join the International Brigade, only to be labelled a spy and flung into jail. Guy hoped the Catalans were less suspicious these days, despite their on-going dispute with Madrid over independence. He had no wish to spend the rest of his holiday in prison.

Figueras was the birthplace of Salvador Dali, the surrealist painter who had left his mark on the world far beyond Catalonia. Dali was not Corelli, of course. He could not have painted *Girl with earthenware jar* if he'd tried. The subject was far too conventional. He would have distorted the jar, as well as the girl, turning both into something beyond the comprehension of mere mortals. To appreciate Dali, one had to be on his artistic wavelength. Few people were, and that's what made him so special.

Yet the Spaniard had come up with a phrase that had implanted itself in Guy's memory and refused to go away. He had spoken of "hand-painted dream photographs". Was that not precisely how Guy had managed to create the girl with the earthenware jar? He had never seen a photograph, let alone the original, yet had conjured up a mental image realistic enough to convince Max, and possibly others, that he was writing about a genuine work of art. The experience was more than dreamlike; it was, as his colleague in the ad. agency had observed, quite surreal.

Van Gogh, portrayed by the Nazis as 'degenerate', was also inclined to fantasise. In one of his more lucid moments, he declared that "painting comes to me as if in dreams". What would Dr Freud have made of that? There was not much sex in a sunflower. At one time, the Dutchman had lived just up the road (if measured in country kilometres) in Arles. For a couple of months in 1888, he shared a house with Gauguin whose style Schulman had compared to Corelli's.

Both were drawn to Provence by the harsh light which intensified colour and gave paintings an extra dimension. The pair had been drinking together – and probably arguing – the night Van Gogh sliced off part of his left ear. That was too much for Gauguin, already feeling the strain of living under the same roof as a madman. Two days later, he packed his bags and returned to Paris. Not long afterwards, Van Gogh went completely round the bend and had to be confined to a lunatic asylum. While out for a walk one day, he shot himself.

Guy felt some affinity to the Dutchman and not just because the artist was his age when he died. One of Van Gogh's paintings, of himself on the road to Tarascon, had mysteriously disappeared after being stored in a salt mine for safe keeping during the second world war. Had it been stolen and sold to some private collector or would it reappear one day, just as Guy's imaginary picture had turned up in Grenoble? And, if it did, would it be the original or a fake? The world of art was full of counterfeit pictures and the people who sold them.

The Yellow House in Arles, where Gauguin did the cooking (he couldn't stomach his host's culinary efforts) and sunflowers sprouted almost daily, no longer existed, alas. It had been damaged by Allied bombers during a raid in 1944 and had to be demolished. A year later, on the very day Hiroshima was reduced to a heap of radio-active rubble, the world's remaining stock of *helianthus vangoghii* also came under fire. *Six Sunflowers,* owned by a wealthy Japanese collector, went up in flames when his home near Osaka was attacked and set ablaze. Who the hell wanted fifteen versions of that god-dammed sunflower, anyway? Guy saw no point in going to Arles – a two-hour journey by train – simply to pay homage to a one-eared Dutchman who had failed to sell a single painting during his lifetime.

Homage to Catalonia was another matter. One morning, after breakfast, he took the train to Figueras, now restored to something like its former glory. The whole town reeked of Dali, even more so now that a fortune teller had claimed to be his daughter. The bewhiskered old chap had been dug up and subjected to a DNA test. Such indignity! Such anti-climax! The test showed that Mother was not one of his conquests or, if she was, the coupling was unproductive. The daughter's crystal ball, it seems, may have been clouded by avarice.

Guy was at the graveside, thinking more about lunch than art, when he noticed a priest hanging about nearby. Not loitering with intent, he hoped. The man of God was wearing a long, black soutane and could not have been much older than Guy himself. Was he one of those priests who preferred little boys or did his tastes extend to the female of the species? Guy hoped it was the latter. He was allergic to queers, especially those masquerading under the cloak of religion.

"Buenos dias, señor," the priest said, catching his eye.

"Buenos dia," Guy replied. "¿Habla inglese usted?"

"A little," the priest testified. "Probably better than I speak Spanish."

"You're not from this part of the world?"

"No. Like you, I am a visitor."

Brother Alphonse introduced himself. Hardly yer average priest, thought Guy. A tad under six foot, well-built, with blue eyes and fair hair, he would not have been out of place on the rugby field. Despite his reservations about men of the cloth, Guy warmed to him.

"Are you here to absolve the departed from his sins?" he asked.

"That would take far more time than I have to spare," Brother Alphonse replied.

Guy chuckled and said: "You can find time to join me for coffee, I trust?"

"I'd like that very much."

Guy led the way to a small café. They sat outside in the sunshine, savouring the aroma of freshly-ground coffee and watching the people strolling by. Most appeared to be locals, grown fat and complacent on the revenue generated by the town's most famous son. Guy was relieved that the priest had an eye for the ladies. Many smiled coyly as they walked past, others made the sign of the cross. One or two, possibly lesbians battling with a hot flush, scowled and looked the other way. Miserable bitches, thought Guy. What they needed was a bloody good screw, ravished by somebody able to make the earth move and teach them the error of their ways. A priest, maybe. He himself had once enjoyed a brief liaison with a woman who later took the veil. She was no novice, even before she became a nun. He ordered two *café con leche*.

"Forgive my ignorance, father," he said when the waiter had gone, "but which Order do you belong to?"

"I'm a Benedictine," the priest replied. "We have a monastery a few kilometres down the road, at Montserrat. I'm staying there for a short break."

"I hope your flock will not take advantage of your absence?"

"I'm sure they will but I shall make them pay for their sins when I get back."

"And where's that?"

"Briançon. A small town in France, not far from Grenoble."

Grenoble! Was he never going to shake off the legacy of *The Cartesian triangle*? The spirits of dead Nazis, buzzing like angry wasps whose nest had been disturbed, seemed determined to pursue him wherever he went.

"Does your family come from there?" he asked.

"Not exactly," Brother Alphonse replied. "I was born in Dresden, in what was then East Germany."

"So you are German?"

"Yes."

"How come you live in France?"

"My parents managed to escape shortly before the regime collapsed. We wandered around Europe for while, before settling near Grenoble."

"You never thought of going home?"

"France is our home," the priest replied. "I grew up and went to school there. My parents still speak German, of course, but we like to think of ourselves as Europeans."

"What about the French? Do they think the same way?"

"Most of them do. Obviously, there are some who won't let us forget the past but on the whole we are made to feel welcome."

"Refugees can't always rely on such a friendly reception," said Guy.

"No. We were lucky. We arrived before migrants began to flood in from the Middle East. Attitudes have hardened since then."

Something about the priest – the set of his jaw, perhaps – suggested that he also had a hard streak. A man who would not hesitate to put the boot in, on the rugby field or anywhere else. Not a man to tangle with.

"What prompted you to join the priesthood?" Guy asked.

"Who can say? I heard the call and answered it."

"I fear I'm not of your faith, father," said Guy. "Or indeed any faith."

"That is not important," the priest said. "The main thing is to remember we're all human beings. You must learn to love your enemies."

"I've got plenty of those!" Guy confessed, as the waiter arrived with the coffee.

"Haven't we all? I often think God must spend his entire day sowing dissent among the faithful."

"Couldn't you persuade him to take a day off occasionally?"

"Which day? Friday, Saturday, Sunday? The Almighty comes in many guises."

"Too many. The world would be a better place if there were fewer gods to stir up trouble."

"I quite agree, my friend. But even if there was only one religion men would still find a reason to kill each other. That's the nature of the beast, I'm afraid. What do you do for a living, by the way?"

Guy told him about *The Cartesian triangle*. Brother Alphonse listened attentively and then said: "You must meet the curator of our museum. We have a large collection of paintings and Brother Peter is very knowledgeable."

"Would he know about Corelli?"

"If anybody does, he would."

Guy was jubilant. He had come to the south of France to put the girl with the earthenware jar behind him for a while. Now here was a chance to solve the mystery.

"When can I visit?" he asked.

"We are open every day. If you like, I will have a word with him and tell you're coming."

"That would be more than kind," said Guy. "I'm here for another few days, so I'll try to fit in a visit later this week."

"Ring first," the priest advised. "Then he can look after you properly.

Chapter VIII

Guy returned to Perpignan, elated by the prospect of pursuing his enquiries with the help of the church. He immediately set about planning his trip to the monastery, said to be the holiest place in Catalonia. He phoned the curator and was delighted that Brother Alphonse had been as good as his word. Brother Peter was expecting his call. The following morning, with only a day or two left of his holiday, he set out for Montserrat.

He crossed the border by train once again, then took the cable car the mountain to the monastery. The original structure, dating from the 11th Century, had been destroyed by the French during one of Catalonia's battles for independence. The monks had rebuilt it and today it stood as a monument to Catalan culture. Not so much a monastery, Guy thought, as a tourist complex with an hotel, cafés and even a railway. As an atheist, he was humbled by such a magnificent tribute to blind faith.

Set high up in the hills, some 4,000 feet above sea level, it was noticeably cooler than down on the coast. Guy was glad he had brought a pullover with him. Hidden among the rocks that towered above the site were caves once occupied by hermits. During the Franco years, many Republicans had sought refuge there. The ancient grottos must have provided an ideal hiding place for those seeking to escape the wrath of the fascists in Madrid.

Brother Peter, a jovial, rotund priest who reminded Guy of Friar Tuck, was waiting for him. He bustled towards his visitor, smiling broadly.

"Welcome to Montserrat," he said, shaking Guy's hand. "Brother Alphonse has told me about your book. How can I help?"

Guy once again recounted the origin of the girl with the earthenware pot. How many more times would he have to repeat the story before the imaginary canvas revealed its secret?

"We don't have any Corellis, I'm afraid," the curator said. "Most of our paintings are home-grown. From what I gather, Corelli spent much of his time in Africa. But your story is entirely plausible."

"Except, of course, that it's also entirely fictional."

"That is not going to deter those who traffic in the spoils of war," the monk said. "They follow up every clue, even if they find only red herring."

"And somebody thought they saw a clue in my book?"

"That seems the most likely explanation. There's no shortage of collectors willing to pay good money for paintings that cannot be sold on the open market. Of course, they can never display them in public. They just gloat over them in private."

"How pathetic," said Guy.

"Where would the church be without these little flaws in human nature?" the priest asked with a smile.

He took Guy's arm and propelled him gently towards the gallery. Guy was overwhelmed by the collection of French, Italian and Catalan paintings. Not since visiting Argentina some years previously had he seen so much art in one place. There, dramatic pictures of life in South America filled every plaza and shopping mall. Ironically, one of the biggest showcases was outside the main cemetery in Buenos Aires where artists gathered to display (and hopefully sell) their work. The monastery's pictures, although stunning, tended to be more predictable. This was, after all, the home of Benedictine monks, not a gallery for the avant garde.

"What a magnificent collection!" exclaimed Guy, hoping to impress the curator with his enthusiasm.

"We like to think so," the priest replied modestly.

"Where do they all come from?"

"Oh, here and there. The faithful are generous benefactors."

Guy wondered how to approach the subject of Nazi loot. The Catholic church still had a lot of questions to answer about its links to the Hitler regime. Those questions included how much it knew about the paintings and other works of art plundered by the Gestapo. He decided to come straight to the point.

"Have you ever been offered a picture suspected of being looted by the Nazis?" he asked.

"Not to my knowledge," the priest replied. "But there's still a lot of them around. Many of the paintings stolen by the Gestapo were purloined by those who knew where they were hidden."

"Poetic justice, you might say," remarked Guy.

"Divine retribution, maybe?"

They moved slowly around the museum, admiring the works on show, while the curator explained their provenance. He was, as Brother Alphonse had foretold, extremely knowledgeable.

"We've had our own problems with looters," he said. "Many centuries ago, the Moors tried to get their hands on our Virgin."

Guy was tempted to make some ribald remark about the beast with two backs but managed to hold his tongue. *Othello* was for the theatre, not a monastery in the hills of Catalonia.

"We hid her in a cave – not unlike the Nazis and their plunder – and today she is on display once again."

"In the museum?" asked Guy.

"No. She has a case of her own, behind the altar," the priest said.

The virgin of Montserrat, a bit of wood imbued with mystical powers, was – according to canonical wisdom – made by St Luke. But as all but the most credulous papist knew full well, science had demolished that theory. Carbon dating had shown her to be a lot younger than the church would have the faithful believe. She was probably only about eight hundred years old, not a couple of thousand. The Black Virgin of Montserrat nevertheless retained her position as patroness of Catalonia.

Guy was longing to ask the priest about the picture that had prompted his visit – the real one, not his imaginary canvas.

"Forgive me for asking this, father," he said, choosing his words carefully, "but I wonder if, during your pastoral duties, you have ever picked up a clue about the fate of Corelli's girl with the terracotta urn?"

"Picked up a clue?"

"Well, somebody's conscience may be troubling them. They may have dropped a hint about what might have happened to her. "

The priest smiled. Here was a heathen asking a man of God to break the seal of the confessional.

"Most Nazis were not Catholics," he said. "The only time they went near a church was to plunder it. And many had died before I was ordained. I can only say, may God have mercy on their souls."

Guy realised he had pushed the monk too far, trespassing on religious territory. He would never make a diplomat. As he struggled to recover from his faux pas, they were joined by Brother Alphonse.

"I heard that you had arrived," the German said, taking Guy's hand. "I'm sure Brother Peter has been taking good care of you."

"He has indeed," said Guy.

"We were just talking about the trade in missing masterpieces," the curator said. "The ones that never reach the saleroom."

"All too lucrative, I'm afraid," Brother Alphonse confirmed. "There is a well-established market for stolen works of art."

"Where do the buyers meet?" asked Guy.

"They don't. That would be far too risky. Most deals are arranged through a third party, either in person or over the telephone."

"Nobody in their right mind would use the internet," the curator put in. "They'd be tracked down and arrested within hours."

"The phone's not very safe, either," the German added. "Not with the Jews and the NSA listening to every word. Of course, you can't just pick up the phone and make an offer. Your credentials have to be established, so to speak."

Guy wondered where the priest had acquired his knowledge of murky dealings in the art market. Not at a monastery in Catalonia, that's for sure.

"It's a bit like a secret society," the curator said. "Only run on criminal lines."

"Sounds like the Mafia to me," said Guy.

"Could be," the monk agreed.

"The pictures themselves must change hands somewhere along

the line," said Guy. "Do you know where?"

"From what we understand," the curator said, "there is a clearing house somewhere in Switzerland."

"Switzerland?"

"Don't sound so surprised, my friend. There is more to Helvetia than a few bars of chocolate."

An order for two copies of *The Cartesian triangle* for a start, thought Guy, not to mention British Airways flight 361 to Geneva.

"Chocolate – and a lot of Russian money," the German added. "Enough to buy our modest collection many times over."

"Are you planning to sell it?" asked Guy.

"No," Brother Peter declared. "And we don't intend to let thieves help themselves. Our security arrangements are more than adequate."

Brother Alphonse nodded in agreement.

They concluded their tour of the museum and made their way back to the curator's office. The priest ushered Guy and his fellow Benedictine inside and took a small bottle from a drawer.

"I'm sorry we couldn't show you any Corellis," he said, "but perhaps I can offer you something by way of consolation? A liqueur named after our Order."

"That would be most welcome," said Guy.

The curator filled a small glass and offered it to his visitor. Guy waited for him to fill two more and, after a toast in Latin, they drank to St Benedict.

"And let us not forget Signor Corelli," said Brother Alphonse, raising his glass again. "Or the charming young lady with the terracotta pot."

Chapter IX

It was raining when Guy arrived back at Gatwick. Not the kind of light drizzle that dampened spirits on a day out but the sort of heavy downpour that often marred Wimbledon fortnight. The type of monsoonal rain that, if the prophets of doom were correct, threatened to wipe out the Maldives, and possibly Gatwick itself. At least it would solve the water shortage in the south-east and pre-empt another hosepipe ban. Global warming had its positive side, whatever the effect on penguins and polar bears. He took the train to Victoria, then the Tube to the Embankment, thence to Blackheath. He was home, if not exactly dry.

Tea. That was the one thing he missed in Perpignan. The Frogs knew how to make coffee but the secret of a good cuppa had somehow eluded them. He put the kettle on and looked around for something to eat. As usual, the cupboard was bare. Intentionally this time, as he had eaten everything worth eating before leaving for France. Now he would have to go shopping again. "To do good work," Van Gogh had written to his brother Theo from Arles, "you have to eat well, be well housed, have a screw from time to time, smoke your pipe and drink your coffee in peace." Guy was not going to argue with that. But first he would check the mail and see if anybody had phoned while he was away. The screw could wait.

The mail was uninspiring. Junk, mostly. How did the originators of this garbage obtain his address? He was not the hapless victim of a county court judgment and had ticked all the boxes instructing those with whom he had done business not to share his personal data. So how come they were able to pester him? He would have to send them an email and try to stop this blatant invasion of his privacy. The telephone was more productive. A message from a woman in Greenwich, inviting him to address the local literary society; another from Sergeant Matthews at Scotland Yard, asking him to phone.

"We've managed to identify your friend," the detective said when Guy returned his call. "A most interesting gentleman."

"In what way?"

"From what we have been able to ascertain," the copper said, hedging his bets, "he was a Russian citizen named Alexei Bukharov, wanted for a string of crimes throughout Europe."

"Good lord! What sort of crimes?"

"Everything from fraud to dealing in stolen antiquities. He seems to have had a great many irons in the fire."

"How were you able to track him down?"

"Through his fingerprints," the sergeant revealed. "We sent a copy to Interpol and they responded almost immediately. He'd left his dabs all over the place."

"That was very careless of him."

"Arrogant, too. It suggests that he did not expect to be caught."

"Have you any idea where he lived?" asked Guy.

"He spent most of his time in Switzerland, it seems. He had a house there but moved about all over the place. One day in Geneva, the next in Paris. He must have spent a fortune on air fares."

The reference to Switzerland was not lost on Guy. BA Flight 361 from Gatwick to Geneva. Would Miss Kovalski be catching a plane to Paris next?

"I guess he followed the money," said Guy.

"More than likely," the copper agreed.

Despite a feeling that he was still under suspicion, Guy was strangely exhilarated. As far as he knew, this was the first time he had enjoyed the company of a criminal. Max, or Bukharov, as he supposed he must now call him, did not strike him as an archetypal villain. He'd had his doubts, of course, reinforced by those portraits on the walls of City boardrooms, but Max gave every impression of being a gentleman. Jewish, of course, but pleasant, charming and erudite. But that's how conmen survived.

"What about the killer's motive?" he asked.

"If we knew that, we'd have something to go on. But may I give you a word of advice, sir? Tread carefully. If any of Mr Bukharov's friends discovered that you'd been in touch with him, or us, your own life could be in danger."

"I can't imagine why anyone would want to kill me," said Guy.

"The sort of people who killed Mr Bukharov don't need reasons. They shoot first and ask questions later."

"A bit like the Wild West," said Guy.

"These days, it's more often the Wild East" the copper said. "By the way, I read your book. You'd make a good member of our special art squad."

Special art squad? Well, that was something else to think about.

Guy thanked the sergeant and said goodbye. The woman in Greenwich could wait. His priority at the moment was to buy some food. He poked around and made a list of what was required to keep body and soul together. Just about everything, in fact. Checking his wallet to make sure he had his credit card (it was embarrassing to arrive at the check-out and discover you had no money), he quietly opened the front door. The Stasi were in the foyer, apparently comparing the various patterns on the carpet.

"Hullo, Guy. Haven't seen you for a while. Been on holiday?"

"Just for a few days. Any visitors while I was away?"

"Didn't see any," the man said. "Where d'you go? New York?"

"No, Cyprus," Guy lied.

Cyprus, where the Crusaders stopped on their way to convert the Moslem hordes. Where Greeks and Turks still confronted each other over the barbed wire. Where criminals from all over the former Soviet Union came to launder their dirty money.

"Which part?"

Guy had to think quickly. Chances were that this obnoxious little oik had been there. Millions of Britons had, soaking up the sun on flea-infested beaches or drinking beer in sleazy bars.

"Do you know the island?" he asked, playing for time.

"I've been there once or twice," the man said. "Paphos, mainly. You can get a full English breakfast there."

“Seems a long way to go for a bowl of cornflakes.”

“Greek food gives me the willies,” the traveller replied. “All those figs and yoghurt. I like to start the day with something edible.”

“You should try the north,” said Guy, invoking Laurence Durrell's *Bitter Lemons* with a silent Te Deum. “They know how to make a pot of tea.”

“Is that where you were?”

“Yes,” Guy lied again.

“Where abouts? Kyrenia?” the man persisted.

“No. Up in the hills. It's quieter there.” He hoped the Turks had not built a rocket-launching site since Larry's days. “Now, if you'll excuse me, I must get to the shops before they close.”

He made his escape and hurried down the street towards the supermarket.

Cyprus: where Aphrodite had waded ashore near Paphos, probably in search of an early Greek breakfast; where the Romans had built their fortresses and savoured the wine; where EOKA terrorists had fought the British during the colonial era and where all those canned peaches came from.

Cyprus: that should set few hares running, he thought.

Chapter X

Tread carefully, Sergeant Matthews had advised. Who wouldn't after learning that a member of their fan club had been shot dead in the street? They might even look over their shoulder now and again to make sure they were not being followed. Those who could afford it hired bodyguards. The man once thought to have topped the Russian rich-list, Badri Patarkatsishvili, had 120 of them. Why on earth did he need so many? He must have done more than write a book about the plunder of Jewish assets by the Nazis. For the life of him, Guy could not think why anybody should want to kill a humble scribbler who had simply penned a few words about an imaginary painting. But, as the man from the Met. had pointed out, the sort of people who murdered Max Schulman often needed no more than a hunch before pulling the trigger.

One fact was irrefutable, however: since the collapse of the Soviet Union, some 200 journalists had been murdered for writing stories that had upset the Kremlin. Anna Politkovskaya was one of them. She had exercised her newly-restored freedom of expression rather too freely, accusing the president of "having the manner of a secret policeman who habitually snoops on his colleagues". That was seen as pushing free speech well beyond the limits and nobody was really surprised when she was shot dead in the lift at her Moscow apartment. That is usually what happened to people who criticised Putin and his allies. Guy remembered uneasily that he had been a journalist. Some people may have thought he still was.

So, Max - or Bukharov – was not a member of the Schulman tribe. That didn't mean he wasn't Jewish, of course. Thousands of Russian Jews, as well as Christians, had settled in London, just as their forebears had done a century or so earlier. But much had changed since the downfall of the Tsar. Russia was not a member of the EU, so they could not just arrive and set up shop. At the very least, they needed a residence permit. Moreover, until the collapse of the Soviet Union and the emergence of a grab-it-now culture, nobody in

Russia had any money. Now they were rolling in it. They owned everything from newspapers to football clubs. One of those journalists shot dead in Moscow had just named one hundred Russian billionaires. Where had their money come from? The British government had at last been forced to ask them to explain the source of their wealth or take the next plane home, wherever that might be. It was unlikely to get any credible answers. Even the village idiot was not going to say he had stolen it.

Many of the newcomers had brought some of their quaint old habits with them. Guy had lost count of how many had died as a result of feuds originating in Russia. Young, healthy Russians fell down dead as they jogged through the leafy lanes of Surrey. Another gunned down in the street outside his home in Canary Wharf. At least Patarkatsishvili, a Jew from Georgia, had managed to die naturally after a heart attack. So much for all those bodyguards. Boris Berezovsky, a former university lecturer and second-hand car dealer who had fallen on hard times, was found dead in his mansion in Berkshire. He had apparently hanged himself. Was it an accident – or had there been foul play? Conspiracy theories abounded. Then there was Nikolai Glushkov, strangled on the day he was supposed to appear in the High Court to account for all the money he had stolen from Aeroflot, the Russian airline. So if Max Schulman had died with a bullet in his back that was no more than par for the course. Tread carefully? Sensible, if somewhat superfluous, advice.

Chapter XI

Guy was in philosophical mood as he walked up the hill from the station towards the heath. Why, he wondered, did poor Vincent's daubs command such phenomenal sums when, during his lifetime, he had failed to sell a single picture? While millions battled with poverty to feed their children, a handful of obscenely rich people spent fortunes on paintings worth little more than the frames that surrounded them. Not so much a tale of two cities – the Dover coach in Dickens' novel had creaked and rumbled through the mud as the horses laboured up Shooter's Hill, a mile or so to the east – but of two worlds. Were the rich really connoisseurs of art or did they just like to flaunt their wealth? The answer was patently obvious. The nouveau riche, especially, were sitting ducks for the silver-tongued highwaymen of the saleroom. They deserved to be held to ransom. As for the unmade beds and pickled brisket said to represent the pinnacle of contemporary art, Guy had nothing but contempt.

He was on his way to address members the Meridian Society, as the local book-reading group liked to call itself. ("It's a bit of a misnomer, really," the chairman had explained. "Some of our ladies don't know where to draw the line.") That should be interesting, thought Guy. He just hoped they weren't a bunch of pretentious bluestockings or loud-mouthed feminists, spoiling for a fight over a few words deemed to be politically-incorrect. With any luck, one or two might actually read books and be persuaded to buy a copy of *The Cartesian triangle*. At least the talk would earn him some publicity, provided somebody remembered to write a report for the local rag.

His thoughts returned to the painting at the heart of the matter. He was still trying to reconcile the *Girl with earthenware jar* with Corelli's *Girl with terracotta pot.* A minor labelling discrepancy – or was there more to it than that? Countless paintings had been touched up or scraped down to reveal something that was not visible when the picture left the artist's studio. Many a hidden drawing had been revealed by X-ray or the skilled hand of a restorer. Did the real painting contain a clue -- a cryptogram, as the spooks at Bletchley Park might have said -- that pointed to a crock of gold? If so, it seemed probable that grandfather Schulman had taken the secret to the grave.

He reached the hall, an ornate building dating from late Victorian times, where he was to address the multitude. Two women, both slightly older than himself but exuding the kind of vitality that bespeaks a healthy bank balance, stood by the door, chatting. One of them, a platinum blonde in a Dior skirt and blouse, smiled affably as he approached.

"Mr Chandler?" she enquired. "I'm Tanya Rosenbaum. We spoke on the phone."

"We did indeed," said Guy, taking her hand.

"I'm so glad you were able to step in at such short notice," she said. "We are all very grateful."

"My pleasure, I can assure you."

"I'm sure it will be ours, too." She turned towards her companion. "May I introduce our membership secretary, Amanda Scott-Hopkins?"

Amanda Scott-Hopkins, a sultry brunette in a pair of well-cut and probably very expensive jeans, smiled and squeezed his hand for a fraction longer than was strictly necessary.

"Welcome to our little gathering," she purred. "It's not often we have the chance to meet a real, live author."

So, the ladies were not fearsome bluestockings, after all. To judge by the reception committee, one or two might even sport a pair of black fishnets. He allowed himself a moment of fantasy.

"What would you like me to talk about?" he asked.

"Whatever you like," said Tanya. "Only don't make it too literary. We are not intellectuals."

"Try to sex it up a bit," suggested Amanda, "like one of Mr Blair's dossiers."

At that moment, Guy was thinking more of Van Gogh's letter to his brother than Blair's porkies about Saddam Hussein's mythical weapons of mass destruction. "To live well," the artist had written, "one needs a screw from time to time." Had he been talking about tobacco or something more life-enhancing? He smiled at Amanda Scott-Hopkins and wondered what sort of legs the blue jeans concealed.

Tanya led the way inside and invited Guy to sit next to her at the table in front, facing the members. She rang a small bell and called the meeting to order. The ladies fell silent. There were about thirty or so, perhaps three dozen, all trying to look their best, some with the help of Oxfam. Their ages ranged from about forty, Guy guessed, to a couple of distinctly elderly matrons of seventy or thereabouts. Yuppies they were not. Amanda, in the front row, crossed her legs and managed to appear both decorous and seductive. Despite the chairman's assertion that they were not highbrows, they all looked ferociously intelligent. He scanned their faces for signs of latent dissent and was relieved to note that none appeared to be a member of the awkward squad. The ladies were clearly too well-bred to engage in a shouting match, especially with a guest. After a few preliminary words about the dire state of public libraries, Tanya introduced "our speaker". The ladies applauded politely and Guy rose to his feet.

He was the only man there and felt thirty pairs of female eyes sizing him up. His reputation, both as author and speaker, was on the line. Try to sex it up a bit, Amanda had advised. He could do that easily enough by recounting the sequence of events following his meeting with Schulman. The dilemma was how much to reveal. He did not want to suggest that he was somehow mixed up in murder. It was all too easy to tar oneself with the brush of suspicion. One day, perhaps, when the mystery had been solved (if it ever was), he would feel free to talk about it. In the meantime, it was perhaps wiser to say nothing. He spoke of his career as a writer, throwing in one or two anecdotes about his previous job as a journalist, before moving on to *The Cartesian triangle*. The aim of the talk, after all, was to sell a few copies.

There were some uncomplicated, innocuous questions – he was glad that nobody probed his knowledge of art too deeply – and the ordeal was over. A cup of tea materialised from somewhere. As he sipped it, three or four women approached shyly, each clutching a copy of *The Cartesian triangle.* Guy signed them with a flourish. The ladies blushed and thanked him profusely. "Just remember it's fiction," he told them.

Amanda Scott-Hopkins lingered nearby, ostensibly talking to another member but casting meaningful glances in his direction. Her body language told him she was ready, willing and available. He was about to join her when Tanya cornered him.

"That went down very well," she said. "The members were most impressed. They have asked me to invite you again."

"I'd be happy to oblige."

"When's your next book coming out?"

"Not until I've written it," quipped Guy.

"You could always give us a preview."

"I don't think my publisher would appreciate that very much."

"Why not?"

"Because if people knew what the book was about nobody would buy it."

"Oh, I see!" said Tanya. "I hadn't thought of it in those terms. How are you getting home, by the way? Can I give you a lift?"

Guy thought it more likely that the totty in the blue jeans could achieve that without much effort. He nevertheless forced himself to be polite. The ladies were, after all, his ambassadors. He could not afford to upset them, especially the chairman.

"That's very kind of you," he said. "But as I walked here it won't hurt me to walk home again."

"I wouldn't dream of letting you," Tanya replied. "You must be tired out, poor thing. Come on, my car's outside."

He caught Amanda's eye and gave her a resigned smile. Maybe next time. He hoped she understood.

Tanya led the way to her car, the latest model Mercedes coupé.

"Hop in," she said, opening the door and slipping into the driver's seat. "I hope you don't scare easily."

She switched on the engine and, after a quick glance into the mirror to check her make-up, pulled into the traffic. As they headed towards the heath, Guy realised they were going in the wrong direction.

"I live just down the road," said Tanya, reading his thoughts. "If you can spare a few minutes, I'd like a chat."

Was this the start of another adventure or was the lady a bluestocking, after all? He would soon find out. Que sera sera.

The Rosenbaums' house, on the Greenwich side of the heath, was a large, detached structure with a short drive and well-kept garden. A row of evergreen shrubs kept inquisitive eyes at bay while from under the eaves peeped a burglar alarm. Guy felt slightly overawed by the obvious wealth of his new friend. His poky little flat would not even have made a summer house in her back yard.

Tanya parked the car – abandoned would be a better word – and opened the front door; a real, wooden door with Georgian panels, not one of those plastic things that defiled porticos elsewhere.

"Welcome," she said, ushering him into the lounge. "I'm afraid we are all alone. The family is away for one reason or another."

The room was light and airy and smelt vaguely of polish. The furniture alone must have cost more than Guy would ever earn from his writing. A three-piece suite upholstered in leather, an occasional table, a well-stocked bookcase and various other bits and pieces. Three or four modern pictures, originals as well as prints, adorned the walls. An open staircase led to the first floor. Tanya indicated the sofa.

"What can I get you to drink?" she enquired.

"Nothing, thanks. Not after tea."

"Meridian tea does tend to cloy the palate," she conceded. "I hope it has not spoiled your appetite, though."

She kicked off her shoes, revealing scarlet toenails, and sat down next to him on the sofa. As she did so, her hand casually brushed his thigh. A frisson akin to an electric shock made him catch his breath.

"What does your husband do?" he asked, his mouth unusually dry. "Something in the City, I assume."

"I'm not sure what he does," said Tanya. "He spends most of his time in Russia, so it's best not to ask."

He noticed that the top button of her blouse had mysteriously slipped its mooring, providing an unimpeded view of female flesh. For a woman no longer in the first flush of youth, she was in remarkably good shape. He wondered how much time she spent at the gym.

"Anyway, I didn't bring you here to talk about my husband," she said. "As you have probably guessed, we Rosenbaums are Jews. You therefore won't be surprised to learn that your book rang all sorts of bells."

"Don't tell me the girl with the earthenware jar is a long-lost family heirloom?" he said, relieved that the conversation had taken a literary turn.

Tanya looked baffled.

"What makes you say that?" she asked.

Guy hesitated. He did not want to reveal matters that he had so far managed to keep secret; Bukharov's murder, his trip to Spain, his contact with the fuzz. Least of all did he want to mention Miss Kovalski.

"Oh, nothing in particular," he said. "I was just thinking of somebody I knew."

"I hope it wasn't that sexy little bitch Amanda Scott-Hopkins. I saw you looking at her."

"There's no harm in looking," said Guy.

"Take my advice: don't let her get her hands on you. Her husband's in the Navy and she suffers from night starvation."

"Has she tried Ovaltine?"

"She's tried everything else, as far as I know, up to and including the first sea lord. Are you married, by the way?"

"Only to my work."

"All work and no play . ." she said, taking his hand and placing it on her breast. "The creative spirit needs a little encouragement from time to time."

Guy bowed to the inevitable and tried to forget Amanda Scott-Hopkins. The elder woman had won the day. Her scent alone aroused desire. Unhooking her bra, he ran his fingers over her nipples. They were supple and resilient. Real flesh, not silicon. Her own hand wandered towards his fly,

"Not so fast," said Guy, pushing it away. "There's plenty of time."

He found her mouth and they enjoyed a long, erotic kiss. By the time they paused for air, Guy had a hard on that would not have disgraced a stallion at stud. He was now anxious to consummate this encounter without delay and so, it seemed, was she. Tanya Rosenbaum was not short of passion. She straddled the author with the ease of an experienced woman and, having been satisfied, demanded more. As they writhed in ecstasy, Guy slipped and fell to the floor, pulling Tanya on top of him. Eventually, the pair of them lay on the carpet, exhausted.

"I'm so glad you didn't say you loved me," she murmured. "I hate hypocrisy. It's far healthier just to admit a bit of animal lust."

"I couldn't make love to a woman I didn't like."

"Well, that's nice to know. Now, don't fall asleep. I want to talk to you."

She picked up her knickers and, kissing him lightly on the cheek, got to her feet.

"Excuse me for a moment. I must dispose of the evidence."

"By their seed shall ye know them."

"Not in this house. The man who discovered DNA ought to be shot."

"A sentiment shared by Kensington Palace, I imagine."

She hurried towards the bathroom while Guy pulled on his pants and tried to look as though he had not been raped. Were all middle-aged women so accommodating, he wondered? Most of his conquests had been younger than himself. But what did age matter when desire was the driving force? The irony of his own position did not escape him. A young man at the mercy of an older woman. He glanced at the pictures on the wall. Nothing by Dali or Van Gogh, thank goodness. At this precise moment, he had no wish to be reminded of Miss Kovalski.

After a few minutes, Tanya returned, looking fresh and vivacious. She had brushed her hair, renewed her lipstick and changed her skirt for one less crumpled.

"I think it's time for that cup of tea," she said.

As she bustled around the kitchen, filling the kettle and rinsing the teapot, Guy slipped his arms around her and fondled her breasts. For a woman with two children, they still had plenty of bounce.

"Quite a handful," he murmured. "Two handfuls, in fact. We must do this again."

She wriggled free and said: "You have my telephone number."

She made the tea, took two cups and saucers from the dresser and placed a cake on the kitchen table. Then she drew up a tubular steel chair and sat down opposite Guy.

"Now, to business," she said. "I brought you here to discuss your book."

"Really? I thought perhaps you had other matters in mind."

"Pleasure before business, that's my philosophy."

"I was under the impression that in Jewish households it was the other way round."

"Some pleasures can't wait," she said, cutting the cake and offering Guy a slice. "Now, your book: it reopens a lot of wounds among we Jews."

"So I've been told."

"The Gestapo were not just thugs. They stole anything they fancied, from whole factories to old masters. Hundreds of paintings are still missing and nobody knows where they are."

"Somebody must know," said Guy.

"That's true. The question is: how much do you know?"

Guy suppressed his exasperation. The girl with the earthenware jar was driving him crazy.

"I know nothing more than is in the book," he said. "And, as I've already told you, the story is fiction from start to finish."

"My husband is not convinced."

"Your husband?"

"Yes. Didn't I mention I had one?"

"Yes, but.." Guy searched for the right words

"He would very much like to meet you."

"I'm not sure that would be such a good idea in view of..."

"Our little bit of fun?"

"He might not regard it as fun."

"Don't be silly!" laughed Tanya. "He's a man of the world and wouldn't expect his wife to remain celibate while he's living it up in Moscow. Besides, I fully expect to receive a packet of photos from the FSB any day now, showing just how unfaithful he is."

"In that case, I'd be delighted to meet him."

"I'm sure it will be worth your while. He meets a lot of shady people in his business, and.."

She stopped abruptly as the kitchen door was flung open and a young woman burst in, dragging a suitcase. Casting an eye over the couple, she said: "I hope I'm not intruding?"

"Of course not, darling. But what on earth are you doing here? Why aren't you at college?"

"I was being pestered by some snotty-nosed Lothario in second-year drama. I thought I'd come home for a few days to let him cool off."

Tanya laughed and said: "You're not going to get very far if you come home every time somebody pesters you. It's something you must learn to put up with. Isn't that so, Guy?"

"It's the way of the world, I guess. Boy-meets-girl syndrome."

"Only if girl wants to meet boy."

"My daughter Rachael," said Tanya by way of introduction. "She's supposed to studying art at Canterbury."

"Hullo," said Guy, shaking hands. Although still in her teens, the girl was already very attractive, with brown hair and dark, intelligent eyes. He could see why Romeo had been smitten.

"Mr Chandler is the author of the book I was telling you about," said her mother.

"*The Cartesian triangle?* Gosh! I must get your autograph."

"I'm afraid that won't help you with your studies very much," said Guy.

"Mummy says I may learn some history from your book, though."

"She's too kind."

The young woman reached across the table and helped herself to a large slice of cake.

"Haven't you had any lunch?" her mother asked.

"No. Or breakfast. I'm starving."

"Well, you know where the fridge is. See what you can find."

"Any smoked salmon?"

"Try Fortnum and Mason. What's in that suitcase? Not washing, I hope?"

"'Fraid so."

"I hope you don't expect me to do it for you?"

"Of course not. Anyway, I can see you're busy."

"Mr Chandler has just given us a very interesting talk at the Meridian Club," said Tanya. "We're having a quick bite before I run him home."

Guy had to admire his lover's sangfroid. Her composure and quick thinking had saved them from a potentially embarrassing situation. Not even the flicker of an eyelid suggested that this was other than a demure tea party. She would make an ideal spy, he thought. Perhaps she was one already. The Jewish state had agents everywhere.

He drank his tea and finished his cake. Then, looking pointedly at his watch, said: "Well, I must be going. I have some washing of my own to do."

"I'll get my keys," said Tanya, pushing her own plate to one side and hastening upstairs.

Guy, left alone with a young woman barely half his age whose mother he had just laid not more than five yards away, was temporarily lost for words. Fortunately, Rachael came to the rescue.

"Mummy says you've hit on a very touchy subject," she said. "Did you set out to be controversial?"

"On the contrary," said Guy, "I had no idea that a book about stolen art would prove so contentious. After all, I'm not the first person to write about Nazi loot – and my girl with the ceramic pot is not Picasso's Guernica."

"Guernica? Wow! That really was controversial. We discussed it last term."

"And what conclusion did you come to?"

"That if the fascists ever came to power again, I would join the Resistance."

"Then you must make sure they don't come to power. Take a stand. Make your voice heard before it's too late."

"My friends think it might already be too late in places like Hungary."

"I've a horrible feeling they may be right," said Guy.

Tanya returned, flourishing her keys somewhat ostentatiously.

"Shall we go?" she asked.

Guy said goodbye to the up-and-coming art historian and followed the older woman to the door.

"Don't forget my autograph!" Rachael called as they left the house and headed for the car.

Tanya backed out of the drive and with a screech of tyres did a swift U-turn in the busy road. As they drove back towards the town, Guy breathed a sigh of relief.

"That was a close shave," he said. "Five minutes earlier and we might have been caught in a somewhat delicate situation."

"I'll speak to her," said Tanya. "Suggest that she phones before turning up unexpectedly."

"What were you going to say about your husband?" asked Guy.

"Husband? Oh, yes. He meets some shady people in his business and may have some information for you."

"What sort of information?"

"I've no idea. He doesn't tell me everything -- which is probably just as well."

"When can I meet him?"

"Whenever he turns up. That might be next week or next month. At least he always phones first."

"That's very considerate of him."

"It's only to make sure there's enough food in the house."

She turned down the hill towards the station and looked enquiringly at Guy.

"Straight ahead," he said.

They drove in silence for a minute or so until Guy directed her towards his flat. She pulled up outside and smiled at him.

"Thank you for your talk and the entertainment that followed," she said, leaning towards him and offering her cheek.

"Forgive me if I don't kiss you in public," he said, glancing toward his flat. "The Neighbourhood Watch even twitches in its sleep around here."

"You're not scared of a pathetic bunch of curtain twitchers, are you?"

"Not if you aren't. But I'd hate word to get back to your husband."

Unfastening his seatbelt, he kissed her quickly and opened the door.

"Thank you for everything," he said. "I'll be in touch."

She drove off, leaving Guy gazing wistfully at the departing vehicle. How many others had enjoyed her favours, he wondered? Did she regard him as a conquest – or just a bit of rough to amuse her while her husband was away? What did it matter so long as they both enjoyed the experience. As he walked up the path, he glanced towards the twitcher's flat. No sign of movement, so perhaps the man had gone out for the day. He would no doubt find out in due course.

Chapter XII

For some reason, Guy was thinking about South America. Not of the mountains and deserts that filled him with awe, nor of the large steaks that had filled him with delight as he chomped his way across the pampa. Not for him a vegan burger and a plate of sauerkraut. He preferred good, red meat, and lots of it. He felt sorry for the poor souls who allowed the threat of global warming to spoil their dinner. No, he was thinking of the Nazis who had sought refuge in those sympathetic lands south of the Orinoco after the war. Thousands of them, including some of the most notorious, had fled – often with the help of the Vatican – to countries where they could put their crimes behind them and start a new life. While the monks of Montserrat had provided a safe haven for Republicans during the Civil War, the Pope and his acolytes had helped hundreds of wanted men to escape down the ratline organised by the Catholic church. Guy looked forward to the day when the archives were opened and the world could gauge the extent of Rome's collaboration with the enemy.

The fugitives from justice were an impressive lot. Adolf Eichmann, responsible for transporting Jews to their deaths in Poland, was tracked down in Argentina; Klaus Barbie, the butcher of Lyon, discovered in and eventually extradited from Bolivia; Mengele and Bormann, both long-term residents of Paraguay where support for Hitler was a matter of national pride. Even Heinrich Müller, head of the Gestapo, was said to have been spotted there. While most former citizens of the Third Reich had kept their heads down and changed their names, some of the most wanted criminals strutted brazenly around, protected by the German community. They were all dead now, of course, but the malady lingered on. Photographs of the Führer could be found all over the place.

As he stared at the blank screen in front of him, Guy wondered whether there was a story to be extracted from Latin America that had not already been told. After all, people were still writing about Colonel Fawcett who vanished in the Brazilian jungle long before the

Nazis came to power. Why not a few words about the Graf von Spee, who went down with his ship during the first battle of the Falkands in 1914, or about Butch Cassidy and the Sundance Kid who lived in Patagonia before it became fashionable? Their hideout – a small farm house not far from Tierra del Fuego -- still attracted visitors. And was there anything more to say about Che Guevara, shot dead while trying to incite revolution in Bolivia? He needed an idea – something, anything – to get the creative juices flowing again. Since publishing *The Cartesian triangle*, he had written nothing, except a few letters and some advertising copy for Crosbie, Grimshaw and Snape. It was time he stopped thinking about Miss Kovalski and got down to work. The rent would not pay itself.

The question of how the Gestapo disposed of its booty continued to bug him, however. It was unlikely, indeed, highly improbable, that fugitives from justice had managed to take much with them. For a start, most paintings were too big and unwieldy to transport half way across the world and would almost certainly have attracted the attention of those on the lookout for Germans on the run. While Customs officers could be bribed, Jews and other Nazi hunters could not. For most criminals, freedom was more important than a few daubs on a bit of canvas. Smaller items, such as jewellery, had nonetheless been smuggled out of Germany and exchanged for cash in countries where few questions were asked. Many a diamond ring or pearl necklace, snatched from the living or wrenched from the dead, had provided the outlaws of the Third Reich with a smidgeon of comfort as they began their new and often anonymous lives.

Some of the paintings left behind had been placed for safe keeping with friends, many of whom were on the wanted list themselves. Unless they wished to be arrested and charged with theft, the temporary custodians were not going to shout about the plunder in their possession. They dare not risk even putting it on display lest somebody recognise it as stolen property. As time passed, the caretakers died and the spoils of war began to gather dust. That's why so many items kept turning up, exposed to the light for the first time in decades when old houses were renovated and the new occupants cleared attics or rummaged through basements. By then, it was too late to enquire how they got there or where they came from.

Not all long-lost paintings were discovered by accident, however. As Brother Peter had pointed out, there was a flourishing trade in works of art that lacked a credible record of ownership. Some were even displayed in galleries which, despite threats of legal action, refused to part with them. Possession, it seemed, was nine-tenths of the law. Of one thing Guy was quite sure: the *Girl with earthenware jar* was not among them. This was and remained simply a product of his imagination.

As his fingers hovered over the keyboard, poised to respond to the first glimmer of inspiration, the telephone rang. Grateful for the interruption, he pushed back his chair and went into the hall to answer it.

"Mr Chandler?" The voice of Detective Sergeant Matthews of Scotland Yard was instantly recognisable. "We have some news of your friend, Mr Schulman."

"Good news, I hope," ventured Guy.

"Nothing that will restore him to life, I'm afraid," the copper said. "But we've unearthed one interesting titbit."

"Oh?"

"Interpol has discovered that, although he was Russian, Mr Bukharov was travelling on a Maltese passport."

"Maltese?" said Guy. "How on earth did he acquire that?"

"Quite easily, I imagine," the sergeant replied. "If you've got money, you can buy anything in Malta, including the people who issue passports."

"I hope he didn't pay them with fake tenners."

"If he did, they're hardly going to complain. There's so much dodgy currency in Malta they probably wouldn't notice, anyway."

"I suppose he hasn't got a Swiss passport as well?"

"Not as far as we know," the copper said. "But there's something else that may interest you. Our ballistics guys have done a few tests on the bullet that killed him. They've identified it as Russian, probably dating from the Soviet era."

"There can't be much of that around these days," said Guy.

"On the contrary," the sergeant replied. "The Middle East is full of it, as well as old Soviet weapons. Kalashnikovs, mainly, but hand guns, too. It's all too easy to get hold of one."

Guy refrained from pointing out that he had made that very point when the police had first interviewed him.

"Does that mean there's an Arab connection?" he asked.

"Not necessarily," the copper said. "But we can't rule out anything at this stage."

"I don't see Max as a terrorist somehow."

"Nor do we. But somebody may have done. There'll have to be an inquest, of course. I'm afraid you'll probably be asked to give evidence, sir."

"So long as I'm not asked to vouch for his character," said Guy. "I barely knew the man."

"We understand that, sir. But the coroner is bound to ask how your telephone number came to be in the dead man's wallet."

"He can ask but I suspect the answer will not be very enlightening."

"That's his problem, not ours. Fortunately, the main purpose of the inquest is to establish the cause of death."

"I should have thought that was fairly obvious," said Guy. "Shot in the back with a Russian bullet."

"I wouldn't mention that, sir, if I were you. You're not supposed to know until the evidence has been made public."

"Sorry," said Guy. "I'll watch my tongue."

Perhaps the sergeant wasn't such a bad chap, after all. Or was this just a ham-fisted attempt to stitch him up? To put him in possession of facts that an innocent person wouldn't know? Guy recalled Chris Lopata's warning: never trust a copper.

"You're not planning to leave the country within the next few weeks, I suppose, sir?" the policeman said.

“I'm not planning to do a bunk, if that's what you mean.”

“Of course not, sir. But the coroner gets a bit shirty if witnesses don't turn up.”

Guy thanked the sergeant for updating him and walked back to his study. He really ought to have an extension fitted or perhaps invest in one of those cordless phones that people seemed to have nowadays. But either would cost money and damage his reputation as a young fogey. Besides, he needed the exercise. He had even begun to count the steps from his study to the hall so that he could calculate how many calories he used every time the phone rang. He sat down and contemplated what he might say to the coroner.

What could he say? The dead man was a complete stranger to him. Apart from the photograph which purportedly showed his family in Vienna, Guy knew nothing about him. He certainly knew nothing about the fake tenners found in his wallet. Least of all could he explain why Max had been in such a hurry to discuss the imaginary painting portrayed in *The Cartesian triangle.* The picture was clearly at the heart of the mystery, whether forged banknotes were involved or not. None of it made sense and Guy felt drawn ever closer to a murder in which he had played no part. That surely provided the basis for his next novel, not some historical account of Nazis living out their final years in South America.

He stared at the blank screen for a few minutes, then pushed the keyboard to one side. It was time for coffee.

Chapter XIII

The village of Klugersdorf in the Swiss Alps had little to recommend it, other than its location. It was pretty enough, with its neat houses and acres of wild flowers, but isolated and remote, well off the track beaten by generations of hikers and backpackers. Never, as far as was known, had it graced one of those postcards that evoked the tinkling of cow bells or the smell of pine needles in the mountain air. Of cars, there were few; of buses, even fewer. That suited the inhabitants who had no wish to be overwhelmed by hordes of camera-clicking Chinese or rubberneckers from Ohio. They were happy to go about their business, far from the maddening crowds of snow-surfers who flocked to the ski slopes further up the valley. In particular, it suited Alfred Neuberger who lived at the far end of the village and was more than content to keep himself to himself.

Herr Neuberger was German although he neither trumpeted the fact nor tried to conceal it. If any of his compatriots lived in the village, he had yet to meet them. He seldom visited the local shops, just phoned through his order and the goods, mainly food, were delivered to his door. He seemed to have plenty of money and always paid promptly. His credit was good. On the rare occasions he bumped into a neighbour, their conversation was brief and to the point. "Good morning, Herr Neuberger. Will you be taking your easel to the hills today?" The answer was usually in the negative. It was either too hot, too cold, too wet or the clouds were too low. To work properly he needed light.

Alfred Neuberger was a painter, and a very talented one at that. He might have been famous had he not been blessed with a faulty gene that led him to deceive those less talented than himself. Instead of producing works under his own name, Alfred used his skill to churn out fake masterpieces. He was adept at copying the style of painters long dead and could switch from one to another at the drop of a palette knife. He even had a set of special brushes that he used to replicate the strokes of illustrious predecessors. Such was the quality of his work that even the so-called experts had been taken in. They found it impossible to distinguish between his forgeries and the originals. Their failure to spot the difference only increased Alfred's contempt for the world of art.

It could be argued, and no doubt would have been had Alfred ever been taken to court, that he himself did not engage in fraud. He simply trod where others had trodden before. If the fake landscapes and portraits that emerged from his studio were passed off as the work of more famous artists that was no concern of his. Caveat emptor. Let the buyer beware. The trouble was that Alfred had accepted the money. Quite a lot of it, which allowed him to enjoy those small comforts that made life worth living in his adopted village.

It both irked and amused him that, while genuine old masters fetched millions, copies – however meticulous - were generally regarded as worthless. Were not his water lilies as good as Monet's? What made Cezanne so special? Alfred could run up a whole field of poppies in an hour or two. One poppy was very much like another, unless it had been sprayed with glyphosate. As for those sunflowers, Alfred preferred their seeds on his bread. If he had a fault, it was that he lacked originality. He was a superb craftsman but relied on others to come up with the idea. He was, he conceded, the human version of a Xerox machine.

What was the point of art, anyway? Was it, as Van Gogh had proclaimed, simply to tell a story, of peasants eating potatoes or drinking wine in a tavern? Or was it to enable the artist to express his opinion of the human condition by holding up two fingers – or one ear -- to the world beyond his studio? People had been arguing about the purpose of art from the moment a few cavemen amused themselves by painting abstract symbols on the walls of their home in France. These days, to 'decorate' one's home with the products of artistic endeavour was the biggest insult one could hurl at an artist.

And who decided what was art and what wasn't? In most cases, it was what the artist said it was, relying on the self-appointed arbiters of taste to validate his opinion. Gallery owners were not going to challenge the assertion that one soup can was better than another if they thought they could make a bit of money. Money. Ah, yes, that's what art was all about. It not only allowed the rich to flaunt their wealth but had become the ideal means of exchange for money stolen from the state. Criminals from around the world, but especially from the Russian Federation, used paintings to wash their dirty money in public. A few million roubles that strictly belonged to the people were miraculously transformed into private assets when ploughed into an incomprehensible daub at an auction house in London or New York. Not all old masters or modern works of art were genuine, however. Alfred sat back, marvelled at how easily buyers could be persuaded that a bit of old rubbish was a cultural icon, copied it, and pocketed the cash.

But, as many a forger had discovered, there was a finite market for fake landscapes and the like. Nearly all the originals had been authenticated and could be admired and studied – under strict security – in galleries around the world. The most a counterfeiter could hope for was to pass off his work as that of a previously-unknown student in the master's studio. But even that was becoming more difficult as science continued to invalidate bogus claims. These days, the tell-tale signs of fraud were not the style but the materials. No longer could canvas made a month earlier in Shanghai be misrepresented as fabric from a previous century. That little caper could be punctured in the twinkling of an electron. He had tried scratching his work – even applying a thin layer of grime to provide a semblance of age – but to no avail.

Even the surrounds were becoming more of a problem. Alfred preferred to recycle old frames picked up in the saleroom. They, at least, were authentic. In days gone by, the best came from houses with collections of solid, if mediocre, work by artists no longer fashionable. His 'friends' kept an eye out for them but the supply was constantly diminishing as old families died off and newcomers with different tastes, or no taste at all, moved in. Many a family heirloom, once regarded as an infallible sign of artistic sagacity, had been written off as junk and consigned to the scrapheap. Alfred was reduced to forging works by artists who had either been overlooked or whose paintings had gone astray. In particular, he had turned his attention to pictures stolen by the Nazis and which had yet to be recovered. The forgeries were dribbled on to the market with the help of associates in the former Soviet Union.

The inhabitants of Klugersdorf may well have wondered how Alfred was able to support himself, tucked away in the Alps, far from galleries that might exhibit his work. They were indeed curious but none was ill-mannered enough to question him about the source of his income. If they occasionally saw a car or van outside the house, that was only to be expected. Nobody could live by themselves without entertaining a visitor now and again. Once or twice, a woman had been seen knocking at his door but that, too, was unsurprising. Most artists used models from time to time. This one was quite slim and attractive. Not Swiss, but not quite German, either. Whether she removed her clothes strictly in pursuit of art was none of their business.

Alfred himself kept a large and very expensive car in the garage adjoining his chalet. He had acquired the vehicle in part exchange for a superb piece of artwork that an accomplice had managed to offload to a woefully ignorant parvenu in Moscow. The go-between was desperate for cash and Alfred was able to pick up a bargain. It was a pity he couldn't drive. Nobody else in the village had a car that size and the vehicle aroused a certain amount of envy. But vandals were few and far between in this part of Switzerland and the vehicle remained in the garage, unused, undamaged and underpinning his status as a man of substance.

Alfred never mentioned his nationality, even on those rare occasions when he stopped to pass the time of day with his neighbours. All they knew was that he came from Germany, probably from the eastern zone. On most days, he stayed at home, ostensibly to work in his studio. How or where he acquired the oils and canvas that kept him busy was a mystery. The nearest big town where they might be obtained was Bern, the capital, but Alfred had never been known to go there. One thing they did notice, however, was that in recent years many of the cars that stopped at his house bore Spanish or Italian number plates. Once or twice, they had even spotted a Russian one.

Despite projecting an image of inner calm, Alfred Neuberger was a worried man. He had always known that one day he would be exposed and his paintings revealed as fakes. In a perverse sort of way, he even looked forward to that day. Every artist, even those who produced forgeries, craved recognition. Stuck up here in the mountains, he had been denied acclaim. Once unmasked, the world would have to concede that here was an artist of no little ability. But now he was being drawn into a scam that demanded no talent, just a willingness to do as he was told. His Russian friends, who had helped to dispose of his work and make him a wealthy man, had begun to lean on him. Alfred found himself being used to launder money from their other rackets. He didn't like that. Bartering large and expensive motor cars was one thing; laundering illicit funds quite another.

The method was simplicity itself. He would be overpaid for some freshly-created masterpiece, then refund half of the proceeds via a bank in Geneva. The money re-emerged, minus the stains it had acquired along the way and washed whiter than the snow that capped the nearby peaks. Just lately, however, the method had changed. His friends had recruited some new partners and Alfred had been asked – instructed – to pay the funds into an account in Malta. That had raised a few eyebrows. The manager in Bern had questioned him closely but Alfred had managed to convince him that all was above board. Perhaps the man was just going through the motions. Without the tacit approval of banks, money launderers would be out of business. And no transfer meant no fee. It was in everyone's interest that bankers turned a blind eye.

But, having been sucked into the mire, Alfred found it difficult to escape. The shackles that bound him to his benefactors were stronger than ever. He began to fear that one day he might be taken to the cleaner's himself. The Russian mafia did not like backsliders – and he knew what happened to people who tried to double-cross them. Even one of their own, Alexei Bukharov, had paid the price for attempting a spot of private enterprise. He had been shot dead while walking down the street in London. Alfred had read about it in the paper. He had no wish to suffer the same fate.

Poor old Alexei! He thought he had found a missing Corelli. Not that it would have made him very rich if he had. The painting was valuable, certainly, but hardly in the megabuck category. Alfred had always regarded Corelli as a second-rate dabbler who would soon be forgotten. He had seen the picture – once – many years ago in France, when he was still legit and working for the government. He had been on a cultural exchange visit to the Chartreuse region, arranged by the people in Berlin. There he met a man, a fellow countryman, who claimed to be an old soldier. Alfred knew better than to ask on which front he had served; under the Stasi, it paid not to be inquisitive. The man, whose threadbare clothes revealed that he had seen better days, invited him home for a drink. Alfred managed to shake off his minder – all too easily, perhaps – and followed him down a narrow street to a small house with a vine clinging to the front wall. They went inside. The shabby furnishings underlined his host's straitened circumstances.

"So, you are an artist, eh?" the man said, inviting Alfred to sit down. He went to the sideboard and, selecting a bottle, poured each of them a large measure of brandy.

"I like to think so," replied Alfred, accepting the drink gratefully.

"In that case, I might have something to show you."

The old soldier hobbled upstairs and returned a minute or so later with the Corelli. He placed it on a chair and stepped back to admire it.

"An impressive piece of work, wouldn't you say?"

"Not bad," Alfred responded diplomatically, "but it's not going to make your fortune."

"Why do you say that?"

"The girl."

"What about her?"

"She's too pretty and her smile too inviting. She's obviously been put there to distract our attention."

"From what?"

"I've no idea." Alfred shrugged. "The urn, perhaps. What do those marks around the rim mean?"

The man looked surprised. He stepped forward and peered closely at the painting.

"I hadn't noticed those before," he admitted. "Probably just decoration."

"Roman numerals on a pot made in darkest Africa?" queried Alfred.

"Why not?" his host asked truculently.

"Because the Romans never got that far. Even Corelli must have known that."

"Artistic licence, that's all."

Alfred put down his brandy and examined the painting closely for a few seconds.

"It looks to me as though the numerals might have been added later," he said. "By a different hand, even. Where did you get it?"

The old soldier, if that's what he was, paused and took a generous sip of brandy. His eyes shone as he smacked his lips.

"It was rescued from the clutches of a family in Vienna," he said. "Jews," he added, spitting out the word with a venom that made Alfred shudder. "We thought it deserved a better home."

Alfred guessed that if the old soldier had ever worn a uniform, it was not that of the Wehrmacht. Black, more likely, with jackboots.

"How much would you say it was worth?" the man asked.

"Nothing," Alfred replied.

"Nothing?" the old soldier exclaimed angrily. "Why not?"

"Because, if it came from where you say it did, you'd never be able to sell it, except on the black market."

His host took another sip of brandy. His eyes narrowed.

"Would you be able to arrange that for me?" he asked with a sly smile.

"I'm afraid not," Alfred replied. "I'm a painter, not an art dealer."

"I'd pay you well," the man said. "Just name your fee."

"Sorry," said Alfred.

"We could go halves. I can't be more generous than that."

"Sorry," Alfred repeated.

Was this a trap? Under the Stasi, one learned to trust nobody, especially a new acquaintance with a shifty manner. Though tempted by the offer, he could not afford to take the risk. The encounter may well have been planned. He recalled how easily he had been able to shake off his minder. Nothing happened by accident in the GDR – or to its citizens abroad. But the episode did put an idea into his head, an idea that would one day bear fruit.

Alfred finished his drink, made his excuses and left. He returned to the East and never saw the painting again. But he had a sharp eye for detail and could probably have reproduced it, had the need arisen.

Alfred's friends were aware that the painting still existed and had been trying – somewhat half-heartedly, in view of their other, more profitable, activities – to track it down. They had even asked him about it. Alfred had professed ignorance. Somehow or other, Alexei had picked up the scent and was trying to trace the picture on his own account. Somebody had tipped off the men in Moscow and they didn't like what they heard. Alexei had broken the code. The penalty for that was death. Alfred had no wish to die just yet, especially for the sake of a painting that he regarded as second-rate.

So, for the time being, the whereabouts of the *Girl with terracotta pot* remained a mystery. Unless somebody had recognised it, which was most unlikely, it had probably been thrown out with his other possessions when the 'old soldier' died, as he surely must have done by now. Even if it did turn up, it was not going to make anybody rich. It was not even worth forging. But Alfred liked to keep some powder in reserve and one never knew when his eye for detail, like that car in his garage, might come in handy.

Chapter XIV

Tanya Rosenbaum had driven to Gatwick, hoping to meet her husband on his return from Moscow. She parked the car, paying through the nose for the privilege, only to discover that his flight had been diverted. Uttering a few unladylike words that revealed a strong grasp of the vernacular, she dashed back to the car and drove hell for leather towards Heathrow, sticking to minor roads to avoid the speed cameras. It would have been far easier to call him on his mobile and tell him to find his own way home. But Tanya was a dutiful wife and appreciated the efforts he made to keep her in the style to which she, and the family, had become accustomed. The least she could do was collect him from the airport. He was already waiting in the arrivals lounge when she hurried in.

"Sorry I'm late, darling," she said, kissing him on the cheek. "What excuse did they offer this time?"

"Something to do with the runway," said Michael, embracing her. "But don't worry, my precious. You're here and we're both in one piece. Would you like a drink?"

"Not if I'm going to drive you home."

"How about a coffee?"

"I wouldn't say no to a cup of tea."

They found a café and casually appraised one another over the teapot. For somebody approaching fifty, he was still as handsome as ever and getting more so by the day. Men improved with age, she reflected, although he could do with a shave. How many women had succumbed to his charms in Moscow, she wondered. He was thinking along much the same lines.

"Have you been behaving yourself while I was away?" he asked.

"Of course. Which is probably more than can be said for you."

"Honestly, darling, you really must stop being so suspicious.

The FSB don't go in for honey traps any more."

"That doesn't stop Russian ladies trying to pick up English gentlemen."

"Only because they want to get their hands on a British passport. Like everything else in Russia, the marriage business is corrupt."

"Then why not offer your services as a makeshift husband? I thought you were supposed to be a businessman?"

"I am. But I already have a beautiful wife who's worth a lot more than a few measly roubles."

Was such flattery an admission of infidelity, she wondered. She could always tell when he had been unfaithful; a courier arrived the next day with a bunch of flowers. On this occasion, she decided to give him the benefit of the doubt.

"In any case," said Michael, "who would want to marry a hard-up Englishman, even for a passport? We are the poor relations these days."

"All the more reason to cash in on demand."

They finished their tea and Tanya led the way to the car. After squeezing his luggage into the boot, they took the motorway and drove leisurely through what was left of the English countryside. At this speed, cameras no longer posed a threat; they were simply part of the landscape. A landscape that comprised largely of motorway signs and acres of concrete, plus the occasional petrol pump and mountain of litter. No wonder the birds didn't sing any more. At last, Blackheath appeared on the skyline.

"What's for dinner?" asked Michael when he had unpacked and changed his clothes.

"Nothing, until you tell me how much you missed me," Tanya responded.

He smiled and slipped an arm around her waist. If she was so keen for a bash between the sheets the moment they arrived home, she had probably not been unfaithful. Or so he allowed himself to be persuaded. Taking her hand, he pulled her towards the settee.

"No, not here," said Tanya, shaking him off. "We'll do it properly, upstairs in the bedroom."

Michael shrugged. The sofa had always been good enough in the past. But women were strange creatures and he had learnt not to argue with them, especially about sex.

"I think you'd appreciate it more if I had a shower first," he said, following her up the stairs.

"You can have one afterwards," she replied. "I don't mind a bit of body odour; it's your body I want."

It had been almost a month since she had opened her legs. Then it was to satisfy lust; now she was hungry for love. Removing her dress, she lay down on the bed. She just hoped that her husband had not picked up some dreadful disease while in Moscow.

*

"What have you been up to while I was away?" asked Michael as they sat down to dinner. She had prepared one of his favourite dishes: sirloin steak (grilled, not fried) with mushrooms, potato dauphinoise and French beans. "Anything exciting?"

"The usual things: cooking, cleaning, feeding the squirrels."

"Can't they find their own nuts?"

"I don't know if you've ever noticed, darling, but there aren't many nut trees in Blackheath nowadays."

"If you say so. I haven't counted them lately." He attacked his steak with gusto. Russian cuisine was not to his taste; nor was the vodka that had turned millions of Russkies into alcoholics. "In my day, gypsies used to eat squirrels. Stewed, or roasted over an open fire. Said to be delicious."

"Fortunately for the squirrels, there aren't many gypsies in Blackheath either these days."

They ate in silence for a while until Michael said: "Did you ever get in touch with that writer chappie – you know, the one who wrote about the Nazis and the missing masterpiece?"

"Yes," said Tanya, avoiding his eye and focussing on her steak. "He gave us a talk at the Meridian Club. I told him you'd like to meet him."

"What did he say?"

"He'd be very happy. I've got his telephone number, if you want to give him a ring."

"Was he – kosher?"

"He seemed genuine enough. Rachael thought he was quite sweet."

"Rachael?"

"She arrived home while we were having a cup of tea. Boy trouble."

"Where is she now?"

"At college, I hope. I told her to go back and stop worrying. Forget boys and start learning."

"I thought boys were an essential part of a young lady's education?"

"Ha! You should know."

Michael finished his dinner and burped discreetly. It was great to be home again and not in some over-priced Russian hotel or nondescript company billet. He poured himself another glass of wine and gazed fondly at his wife. She had taken good care of herself and despite the inevitable ups and downs of marriage he still loved her. They were on the same wavelength and understood one another. His eyes clouded slightly as he wondered how to broach the subject that had been on his mind for some time.

"I'm afraid we may all have to start worrying soon," he said.

Tanya looked startled. Was the FSB on his tail, after all?

"Why? What's wrong?" she asked, putting down her knife and dabbing her lips nervously with the napkin. Her hand trembled as she reached for her wine.

"Nothing that a revolution wouldn't put right," said Michael. "But things are getting pretty tough in Moscow."

"Tim did say it wasn't an easy place to do business," Tanya reminded him.

"I know. But it's not just the marriage market that's corrupt; the whole country is wedded to graft. Everybody expects their cut."

"That's only fair, surely?"

"Yes, if the money reached those who needed it. But it doesn't. It goes straight into the pockets of Kremlin cronies. The poor are as poor as ever, and far less secure. They were better off when the state controlled everything."

He paused to savour his wine and cut himself a sliver of Gruyère. With a touch of grey at the temples, he looked quite distinguished although the strain of working under a corrupt dictatorship was beginning to show.

"There's a political dimension, too," he continued. "People are being flung into jail on the flimsiest of pretexts. You've only got to be labelled undesirable and you can find yourself behind bars. So far, it's only Russians – Pussy Riot and the like – but the day will come when they start arresting foreigners."

"Well, you've done nothing wrong - have you? You're not queer – or a threat to state security."

"You don't have to do anything wrong," her husband replied. "Just trying to turn an honest penny is hard enough. I'm beginning to wonder if it's worth the candle."

Tanya's world began to wobble. Both she and her husband had worked hard and endured long separations to achieve their present standard of living. They hadn't always lived in a big house. Tanya could remember their first home, a two-bedroomed flat in a distinctly unfashionable part of town. She shuddered at the memory. Russia had been good to them - and for them. They ate well, dressed well and had managed to put one child through university. Another was still there, learning about art (and boys). But it all cost money. She was determined not to let her husband throw in the towel without a fight.

"Well, you're not going to resign, are you?" she asked. "Where would you get another job?"

She omitted to say "at your age" but Michael read her thoughts.

"It would be difficult, I know," he said. "And even if I could find somebody to employ me, I don't want to commute into the City every day, packed like a sardine in some over-crowded train. I've reached the stage where I can do without close encounters of the human kind."

He took a mouthful of wine. Full bodied, excellent vintage; he had selected it himself during a tour of French vineyards a couple of years ago. But it had been bought by consorting with people whose ethics did not bear scrutiny – a corrupt elite who would one day bring the whole edifice crashing down.

"We've done quite well, my love, and probably wouldn't starve. But we may have to trim our sails, even downsize and move away from London. It's far too expensive, anyway."

Tanya felt her hackles rise. To her, downsize meant downmarket. It meant exchanging their present home for some anonymous house, even one with four bedrooms, on some equally anonymous estate, far from London. And, after driving a top of the range Mercedes, she did not intend to be seen behind the wheel of a Ford Fiesta. Those days were past.

"You're being defeatist," she declared. "You've been dealing with these people for years and you haven't been arrested yet. Putin can't last for ever."

"I'm not so sure about that," Michael replied. "He's a bit like the Blessed Margaret, determined to go on and on and on."

"Maybe. But look what happened to her."

"Even when he does go, somebody worse may take over," Michael said. "That's when there will be blood on the streets. I don't want to be caught in the middle. I'm not a journalist."

"I've never been quite sure what exactly you do do," said Tanya, sounding slightly exasperated.

"I've often wondered myself," Michael replied. "I suppose you could say I'm a facilitator."

"What does that mean?"

"It means I facilitate meetings between people – Russians, Brits, Israelis – who want to meet one another. A sort of PR man cum business consultant. Nothing very sinister."

"And they pay you for that?"

"Of course. Usually very well."

"Thank you for telling me after all these years."

"I'd always assumed you didn't want to know, so long as the money kept rolling in."

Tanya flinched, hurt by the suggestion that money was all she cared about. That was the sort of remark one might expect from a fascist, not one's husband.

"I didn't ask because I thought it diplomatic not to," she said.

"Your instinct does you credit, my love. It's best not to probe too deeply when dealing with the Russians – at least, not if you wish to see the sun rise again."

Tanya surveyed the remnants of her meal, forlorn and uneaten on her plate. In her family, to waste food was a crime but the possibility that they might have to move from Blackheath had quite ruined her appetite.

"In any case," she said, "where would we go? All our friends are here. I don't want to live next door to a bunch of goys, not with anti-semitism on the rise. We should stick together."

"How about Leeds?" asked Michael with a mischievous smile. "Or Manchester, perhaps?"

"The North? Mushy peas and chip butties? You must be joking!"

"There's always the homeland," Michael suggested.

"And get blown up by the Arabs? No thanks. I'd sooner starve here."

"Let's hope we won't starve anywhere, my precious. I'm just saying the good times won't last for ever. We should prepare for the worst, like Boy Scouts."

"Well, you're not a Boy Scout, so let's not anticipate matters. There's no point in chucking it all in before we have to. Besides, I'm not going to live in a tent."

Michael sighed. He shared his wife's trepidations. He may have been tired of Moscow but he didn't want to move from Blackheath, either. It suited him. He reached across the table and squeezed her hand.

"All right, my little nublick," he said. "I'll keep taking the tablets."

"And the commission," Tanya advised. "In the meantime, you can help me with the washing up."

Chapter XV

The writer chappie had been making good progress with his new novel, even though he did not yet know what it was about. Words were what mattered. He could sort out the plot later, when several thousand of them were lodged safely in his computer. For the moment, he felt like a sculptor contemplating a block of marble. The story was there; all he had to do was chip away until the shape emerged. He just hoped that when it did the plot would not be full of holes, like something knocked up by Barbara Hepworth on one of her off days. He had also been writing ad. copy for Crosbie, Grimshaw and Snape to earn a bit of money. That was always useful, especially at meal times. Hunger, not fame, was the spur.

One morning, when he was toiling away at the keyboard, the phone rang. He was tempted not to answer it lest the caller disrupt his train of thought. He knew how easy it was to lose the thread. Eventually, he walked into the hall and picked up the receiver. He was surprised, and somewhat unnerved, to find himself talking to Tanya's husband.

"My wife has been telling me all about you," said Michael, unwittingly causing Guy's heart to flutter. "You seem to have charmed the literati. I wonder if you'd care to pop over for a chat some time?"

"I'd love to," said Guy, relieved that he had not been challenged to a duel. "Tanya says you may have some information about the art market."

"Possibly, although market is not a word I'd use."

"More a trap for the unwary, I gather."

"Exactly. Why not come on over and we'll have a bite to eat. Would Sunday suit you?"

"Perfect," said Guy.

"You know where we live, of course?"

There was an autumnal feel to the air as Guy made his way across the heath to the Rosenbaums' house. The evenings were drawing in and by the time he arrived twilight had given way to dusk.

He pulled the bell rope and heard a distant chime. While waiting, he wondered who owned the small car parked in the drive. It seemed somewhat out of place, like a clapped-out Cortina in a showroom for Jags. Rachael's runabout, perhaps. A moment or two later the door opened and Tanya appeared. She looked stunning in a pink and turquoise evening dress that was simultaneously modest and revealing. Guy was momentarily struck dumb. To think he had scored with this beautiful creature took his breath away.

"Hullo!" she exclaimed, loud enough for her husband to hear. "Nice to see you again. Do come in."

He followed her into the lounge where Michael was standing with glass in hand, chatting to another guest.

"You remember Amanda, of course," Tanya said brightly.

"Of course," said Guy, thrown into confusion.

What the hell was she doing here? Had she been invited simply to make up the numbers – or to create a smoke screen? The latter seemed more likely. At least it explained the car.

"Her husband's away, sailing his boat somewhere," said Tanya, "so I thought she might welcome a spot of company."

Amanda Scott-Hopkins, looking as seductive as ever in a dark trouser suit, smiled and offered her cheek.

"So, we meet again," she murmured as Guy obliged with a quick peck. Was this part of some elaborate charade? Did she *know?*

Michael put down his goblet and turned towards his guest.

"Glad you could make it," he said, shaking hands. "What can I get you to drink?"

Guy found himself nursing a small sherry and sitting next to Tanya on the settee. With her flesh only inches away, her perfume made his head spin. At the same time, he struggled to keep his eyes off the totty seated opposite whose legs were again concealed by a pair of trousers.

"I read your book," Michael was saying. "An all-too-familiar story among we Jews, I'm afraid." Noting the look of dismay on Guy's face, he added quickly: "I don't mean that in a pejorative sense, of course, but as Tanya has probably told you, many of the artefacts stolen by the Nazis have still not been recovered."

"So I gather," said Guy. "But I very much doubt if *The Cartesian triangle* is going to help you find any."

"What makes you so sure?"

"Because my girl with the earthenware jar is a complete fabrication. She doesn't exist, except on paper."

"Fiction she may be but you'll have your work cut out trying to convince one or two folks in Moscow," said Michael. "They're getting quite worked up about her."

"Oh?"

"As you know, there are some pretty dodgy characters in Russia these days. Unfortunately, I have to deal with many of them during the course of business. That's how I picked up a whisper about the *Girl with the terracotta pot*."

"Whisper?" said Guy. The only whispers he knew came from novels about the secret service in the days when spies monitored the enemy's radio.

"Yes. By all accounts, the real painting still exists. The Mob are trying to get their hands on it. Why, I cannot imagine."

"Maybe they're planning to open a museum of contemporary art," said Tanya. "A sort of Russian version of the Tate."

"Heaven forbid!" cried Amanda. "Where will all those unmade beds come from?"

"Not this house, I hope," said Michael.

"They could always fill the place with fake water lilies," Tanya suggested. "I doubt if anyone would know the difference."

"One of my clients recently paid a lot of money for a picture that turned out to be a fake," Michael divulged. "He's most unhappy."

"And so he should be," retorted Amanda. "I'd be jolly annoyed if I were palmed off with a fake Rembrandt."

"That's not something that's ever going to bother me," Guy confessed, amid laughter.

"Nor me," added Michael, casting a quick eye over the paintings he had acquired on his travels. "Rachael says that, with my taste, I'm never going to make a fortune."

"I'd hang on, if I were you," advised Mandy. "Fashion tends to be somewhat fluid in the world of art. Her views will probably have changed by the time she graduates."

"You must come back in a couple of years and let me know whether I'm in the money."

"Must I wait two years?" Amanda asked coquettishly.

"Yes," Tanya replied. "In any case, I suspect that Rachael will have told him whether he needs to upgrade the security arrangements."

Guy wondered whether the time had come to reveal how he had been sucked into the real, and distinctly murky, world of art. So far, he had not told anybody about his meeting with Max Schulman, a meeting that had opened up a Pandora's box of intrigue and suspicion. Now seemed an opportune moment. Turning to Tanya, he said: "I have a confession to make."

Tanya blanched. Was he about to spoil the party?

"I didn't want to say anything before because I hoped the whole affair would blow over," said Guy. "But perhaps you ought to know that I've been questioned by the police about a murder."

"Murder?" cried Mandy. "Have you killed somebody?"

"Not yet," said Guy. "But a man I met a few weeks ago – a Russian, as it happens – was shot dead as he walked down the street near Marble Arch."

"That's hardly a unique occurrence these days," Michael observed. "A lot of former comrades who fell out during perestroika are still trying to settle old scores. What was his name?"

"Well, he called himself Schulman but the police discovered that his real name was Bukharov."

"Schulman? That rings a bell. There was a well-known family of that name in Vienna before the war."

"That's the one," said Guy. "Do you know anything about them?"

"Only that they were very wealthy and the old boy had an eye for the ladies. He made his money in Africa, I believe."

"Max – Bukharov – told me he'd set up a trading company there. I guess it must have been quite profitable in the days of empire."

"Most European businesses were," said Michael, "until the wind of change blew everything off course. Now you can't even open a corner shop unless you dash the president."

"What happened to all the money?" asked Mandy.

"Nobody knows," Michael told her. "The family – Jewish, of course – was virtually wiped out during the war. Rumour has it that the old boy saw what was coming and put the funds out of harm's way. But where? That's the 64-dollar question."

"If it's only 64 dollars, I can't see what all the fuss is about," said Mandy. "Why not let sleeping dogs lie?"

"Perhaps I should have said 64 thousand dollars, adjusted for inflation."

"Even that wouldn't get you very far these days," Tanya observed.

"Not with you behind the wheel, my love," said Michael.

"You surely don't expect me to buy my clothes at Primark?" Tanya retorted.

"Of course not, darling. But you might occasionally wait for Harrods' sale."

Guy attempted to steer the conversation back to the Schulmans.

"I gather that several members of the family did survive the war," he said. "They might know where the money is."

"I suppose it could be in a safe-deposit box somewhere," conceded Michael.

"What's the point of leaving all that money in a box?" asked Mandy. "You can't spend it there."

"I believe it's known as the feel-good factor," Guy told her.

"I'd feel good if I had a box full of money."

"Maybe it contains the family jewels," Tanya suggested. "Something to fall back on when times got tough."

“Provided that nobody had managed to break in and help themselves,” said Guy.

“It would have to be a pretty duff bank to let a stranger into the vault,” said Michael, “although it does happen. It's a lot easier to bribe the staff than dig a tunnel.”

“Do you remember that film – *The Italian job,* I think it was called?” asked Mandy. “That was about some people who broke into a bank by digging a tunnel.”

“The banks have learned a thing or two since then,” said Michael.

“So have the crooks,” Mandy reminded him.

“If the money was safe, why would anybody be interested in a painting that by all accounts is relatively worthless?” asked Guy.

“I've no idea,” Michael replied. “But there must be something about it that would help to buy more than a few frocks in Primark. I'd watch your back, if I were you, Guy. Anybody who knows anything they shouldn't tends to die prematurely in Russia these days.”

“Fortunately I'm in Blackheath at the moment.”

“That won't save you if you're on their hit list. They obviously think you know where the picture can be found.”

“I do,” said Guy. “It's all in the mind. My mind. The only trouble is that it's driving me round the bend.”

“Why didn't you tell us you were a wanted man?” asked Tanya. “That would have given members something to talk about.”

“I didn't want to alarm you,” said Guy. “The details would only have kept you awake at night.”

“You needn't have worried about that,” Amanda said. “I don't mind being kept awake at night.”

Tanya decided the conversation was heading for dangerous waters. It was time to change course. “Murder, forgeries, the police,” she said. “Whatever next? I think we need something to eat before we all go round the bend.”

She got to her feet and ushered her guests towards the dining alcove. Guy finished his sherry and stumbled after her. Fortified wine on an empty stomach was never a good idea. Amanda smiled encouragingly as they took their seats. Tanya withdrew to the kitchen.

The meal was clearly going to be more than just a bite to eat. The table was set for four, the lighting subdued, the atmosphere intimate. Guy hoped it would not become too intimate and lead to indiscretions he would later regret. He liked Michael and did not want to ruin their friendship before it had really begun. A few white lies to protect the guilty were necessary if it were to succeed.

"I forgot to ask if you were allergic to anything," said Tanya, emerging from the kitchen with the first course: avocado stuffed with prawns.

"Only to old masters and Russian hitmen," replied Guy.

"I can't imagine why anybody would want to kill you over an imaginary painting," said Mandy, delicately stabbing a prawn. "It doesn't make sense."

"Does anything make sense in the world of art?" asked Michael. "I mean, who'd pay millions of dollars to look at three old men playing cards?"

"Three obscenely rich old women, perhaps?" said Guy.

They spooned their way through the avocado – perfectly ripe and neither too big nor too small – and Tanya retired to the kitchen once more. An appetizing aroma of something vaguely exotic wafted towards the dining area.

"I hope you like beef Stroganoff," she said, returning shortly with a covered dish. "It's about the only thing Russian that Michael will eat."

"I like anything that's been cooked by somebody else," said Guy, "but this smells delicious."

"Thank you," said Tanya, handing round the hot plates. "I unfroze it myself."

Guy reflected that beef in sour cream was hardly kosher. In an Orthodox household, such a dish would at the very least have required separate plates. He was grateful that, in deference to their guests, the Rosenbaums were not observing strict dietary rules. Perhaps they didn't anyway and the fridge was full of cold pork. He knew several Jews who ate ham sandwiches – and many a shop that sold them. He noted also that Tanya had prepared vegetables – roast potatoes, fine beans – to accompany the meat, not rice. He'd had more than enough oven-ready meals that consisted more of rice than anything else, except perhaps salt.

"Who was this man Stroganoff?" asked Mandy, helping herself to strips of prime beef as Michael filled her glass. "He must have been a very creative cook."

"I don't think he ever did much cooking himself," Michael informed her. "He was a diplomat in the service of the Tsar."

"Perhaps if he'd ventured into the kitchen occasionally, he would have seen how the workers were exploited and there wouldn't have been a revolution," said Guy.

Amanda paused and, looking at her fellow guest with wide eyes, asked innocently: "You're not a Bolshevik, by any chance? I've always wanted to find a Red under my bed."

They all laughed but it did not escape Tanya's notice that this was the second reference to bed within the space of half an hour. It was time to fire a shot across the bows.

"I hope your bed is not one of the unmade variety," she said. "I can't see any self-respecting man wanting to hide under one of those."

"My bed complies fully with Naval regulations," said Mandy. "My husband insists on that. But, then," she added lightly, "he's never at home to check."

"Are you sure he hasn't installed a bugging device to keep an eye on you?" asked Michael. "We're all suspects now, you know."

Tanya looked at him swiftly. It had never occurred to her that her own husband might be spying on her. After all, the Russians were experts in such matters. Had he picked up their bad habits during his time in Moscow?

"What an extraordinary suggestion!" she exclaimed. "I'm sure Chris would never dream of such a thing."

"Then you don't know my husband!" said Mandy. "That's

exactly the sort of thing he would do. Officers are not always gentlemen."

Was this how marriages began to fall apart? A quip, a jest, that revealed some underlying tension or smouldering distrust. Guy realised he had a lot to learn about the joys of matrimony. At least the only person he knew to be spying on him was the coppers' nark on the other side of the foyer.

"Where is the good ship Lollipop at the moment?" asked Michael. "At sea, I presume, playing hide and seek with the Russians?"

"It's no good asking a sailor's wife," Mandy replied. "They're usually the last to know. The Navy seems to think that, like most women, wives can't be trusted to keep a secret."

So, the bitch *did* know. If she didn't, she had a pretty good idea. Women had a sixth sense about these things. He studiously avoided looking at Tanya.

"How come you're not married, Guy?" Amanda asked him. "Or is that another of your own little secrets?"

"Yes, I keep my wife in a harem," he replied. "She's training to become one of the 72 virgins in Paradise."

"She wouldn't last long in this house, would she, darling?" said Tanya. "She'd fail the test after about two days, I reckon."

"That long?" Michael asked, smiling at his wife's back-handed compliment.

"Are you allowed to visit her?" Mandy enquired.

"Yes, but only on Fridays. The rest of the week I'm free to seek my pleasures elsewhere."

"Today's Sunday," Mandy observed.

Tanya feared the ship was heading for the rocks again. The green-eyed monster stirred in her breast. She had no wish to see her lover snatched from under her nose, especially while under her own roof.

"Now, what would you like for dessert?" she asked, glancing around the table. "Cheesecake or fresh fruit?"

"I think I'll just settle for coffee, if you don't mind," said Guy. "After the Stroganoff, I really have no room for anything else."

"Nor me," Amanda added. "In fact, I'll probably have to go on a diet. I don't want Chris to think I'm pregnant."

"What about you, Michael?"

"I'll settle for coffee, too. The cheesecake can wait."

Tanya withdrew to the kitchen and they soon heard the coffee grinder at work. How much more civilised, thought Guy, than dinner in his own house. There, Sunday-night tea usually consisted of soup and a bit of toast, if he was lucky.

Michael rustled up some petits fours and as they sipped their coffee Guy felt Amanda's eyes upon him. He recalled their first meeting when she had signalled her availability, only for him to be whisked away by Tanya. He didn't want to offend her again.

"Was that your car I saw in the drive?" he asked.

"Yes. I'll take you for a spin, if you like."

"That should take your mind off Russian hitmen," said Michael. "You'll still be dicing with death, though."

"We've all got to die some time," Guy observed.

"Thank you for the unanimous vote of confidence," said Mandy. "I must remember to get the brakes fixed some time, before the Grim Reaper comes touting for business."

They finished their coffee and moved back to the lounge. Mandy casually placed herself on the sofa next to him. Guy felt a tingle of excitement. How had he managed to find himself in such an invidious position – a donkey between two bales of hay? Michael noted his discomfort and smiled knowingly.

After some desultory conversation that avoided any mention of murder, Russian hitmen or fake Rembrandts, Guy sighed and said: "Well, it's getting late. Time I returned to my hovel and let you get some sleep."

"I must be getting along, too," said Amanda. "If I'm not home by eight bells, the officer of the watch will turn me into a pumpkin."

She stood up and, embracing Michael, kissed him fondly on

both cheeks. Michael responded in kind, throwing in a hug for good measure. If the Russians could do it, so could he.

"Thank you both for a wonderful evening," said Mandy. "I've not eaten so well for months."

"Nor me," Guy agreed. "And I'm very grateful to you for filling me in about the Schulmans. It has saved me a lot of hard graft."

"My pleasure," said Michael. "But remember to watch your back, Guy. The Russian mafia does not take prisoners."

The Rosenbaums accompanied their guests to the door. It had been a successful evening, and an instructive one. As they prepared to take their leave, Mandy turned to Guy and asked: "Can I give you a lift?"

"I don't want to put you out of your way."

"No problem. There's not much traffic at this time of night."

"Always helpful when the brakes are a bit dodgy," said Michael.

The Rosenbaums waved goodbye as the pair made their way to the car. Michael closed the door and said: "I hope the poor chap doesn't come to grief."

"He'll have only himself to blame if he does," Tanya replied.

Putting on a brave face, she resigned herself to the fact that on this occasion the younger woman had walked off with the prize.

Chapter XVI

"Which way?" enquired Mandy as she backed the car out of the drive. The last time he was asked for directions he was wallowing in the luxury of a gleaming Mercedes. Now he was a prisoner strapped into the front seat of an ancient Renault.

"Head for the station," he said. "I'll direct you from there."

As they drove across the heath, he glanced at the totty behind the wheel. Not much older than himself, but younger than Tanya, she appeared even more desirable than when he first set eyes on her. The moonlight only enhanced her allure.

"Have you known the Rosenbaums long?" he asked.

"About three or four years," Mandy replied. "Tanya and I are both grass widows so we need a shoulder to cry on from time to time."

"I'm sure you could have found one of those easily enough."

"Not as easily as you might think," she said. "But I keep looking."

They passed the station and the old car began to shudder as it tackled the hill. Mandy quickly changed gear to help it up the slope.

"Left hand down a bit," said Guy as they approached the street where he lived. Mandy smiled and a few seconds later they pulled up outside his flat.

"Coming in?" he asked.

"Only if you promise to be a good boy."

"I never make promises I can't keep."

She turned off the engine and was about to get out when she asked suddenly: "Is it okay to park here? I don't want to get a ticket."

"It's Sunday. Remember? Even traffic wardens like a day off."

"Let's hope they don't start work too early on Monday."

As they walked up the path under the pallid light of a street lamp, Guy glanced briefly at the twitcher's window. Hopefully, the man had gone to bed. One of these days, if he persisted in snooping on his neighbours, he would be taught a lesson he wouldn't forget. Opening the front door, Guy switched on the light and led the way into the lounge.

"Would you like a nightcap?" he asked.

"I'd prefer a pee," Mandy replied.

"After you," said Guy, indicating the bathroom.

While she was absent, he hurriedly tidied the place, straightening the cushions and flicking a few crumbs that had somehow escaped the vacuum cleaner to the floor. He was glad he had made the bed before leaving. Unmade beds were for those who wished to make an exhibition of themselves. He had more practical uses in mind.

"What a sweet little flat," remarked Mandy on her return. She cast a critical eye over the furniture, a mismatch of odds and ends thrown together by a landlord more interested in the rent than the comfort of his tenant.

"Where's your bedroom?" she asked.

"This way," said Guy, taking her hand. He rather wished she wasn't so keen. He enjoyed a bit of a tussle. At the bedside, she yielded to his embrace and they exchanged a perfunctory kiss.

"I hope you're not squeamish," she said, as his hands wandered from her breasts to a more sensitive erogenous zone.

"Squeamish? What on earth makes you think that?"

"Sit down and I'll show you."

More intrigued than perplexed, Guy sat on the edge of the bed and watched while Amanda unfastened her belt and let her trews fall to the floor. As she stood there, with her trousers around her ankles, Guy saw why she chose not to wear a skirt. Her left leg was disfigured by a jagged scar that ran down the inside of her thigh, all the way from her crotch to her calf.

"Oh, my poor darling!" he groaned. "How did that happen?"

"The fox's revenge," said Mandy. "I was out with the hunt one day when the horse suddenly shied and threw me. Unfortunately, I landed on a rusty old plough that had been abandoned at the side of the field."

"How awful," said Guy. "Did you break anything?"

"Only the plough."

Guy ran his finger down the wound which was still red and angry. The doctor had done his best but the flesh had knitted unevenly, leaving a scar like a badly-made zip where the stitches had been.

"Does it hurt?" he asked.

"Not any more."

"You were lucky not to get blood poisoning."

"I did. For a week or so, it was touch and go whether I would survive. The Navy even sent a helicopter so Chris could be at my bedside."

"In hospital, I presume?"

"Of course. I lost a lot of blood."

"What happened to the horse?"

"Oh, he was fine. The hunt caught him and returned him to the livery stables."

"He wasn't yours, then?"

"Heavens, no! A skipper's wife can't afford to run a car and feed a horse."

Mandy was still standing before him, half naked, with her trousers around her ankles, anxiously awaiting the next move.

"Do you still want me?" she asked plaintively.

"Of course I want you!" he exclaimed. "You're a woman, not a china doll. I'm not going to reject you because of a small blemish on one leg."

"I haven't even got blue eyes."

"It's not the colour of your eyes that interests me," said Guy, noticing a single strand of pubic hair protruding from her panties, "but what's between your legs. I assume that survived the ordeal intact?"

"It wasn't damaged, if that's what you mean."

Pulling her towards him, he kissed the upper part of the wound and gently removed the rest of her clothes. As she stepped out of her trews and slipped between the sheets, he asked: "What made the horse shy, by the way?"

"We never found out. Hunt saboteurs, probably. There was a group of them in the next field. They may have used some kind of electronic device to frighten the animal. The police investigated but could find no evidence."

"Bastards," said Guy.

"The police – or the rabble?"

"Both," said Guy.

Taking off his own clothes, he threw them into a heap on the floor and jumped into bed next to her. "Well, Mrs Scott-Hopkins," he said, turning off the light, "let's hope the officer of the watch is not on pumpkin duty tonight."

Chapter XVII

With two scalps under his belt, Guy was in no hurry to acquire a third. It was going to be hard enough juggling the demands of two women, especially when they were friends and lived in the same town. His diplomatic skills, to say nothing of his stamina, would be tested to the limit. But jealousy and lust posed hazards of their own and he would have to proceed with caution. At least neither woman appeared to have been infected with the *#MeToo* virus which was poisoning relationships between the sexes. They understood why women had been put on the planet and rejoiced in their sexuality. They enjoyed a good screw and derived extra pleasure from satisfying men who had not been emasculated by political correctness. Not for them the vicarious sex of a porn magazine or the so-called adult channels on television. They were in it for real.

A couple of days after his post-prandial romp with the compliant Amanda, Guy was returning from the supermarket when he ran into the twitcher. The man was hurrying along on a mission of his own and had apparently not seen the author. He seemed vaguely embarrassed when at last he recognised his famous neighbour.

"Hullo, Guy," he said, stopping for what Guy hoped would be an extremely brief chat. "Been shopping?"

"Looks like it," said Guy.

"I guess your lady friends must be eating you out of house and home."

Guy frowned and said: "What do you mean by that?"

"Come off it, Guy," the man smirked. "Do you think I don't know what goes on in your place?"

"What's that got to do with you?"

"Everybody has a duty to keep their eyes open in this day and age, what with crime and all that."

Guy was seized with anger. Clenching his fist, he took a step towards the man and said: "Listen, chum. If you don't mind your own fucking business, you'll get a smack in the teeth. Understand?"

The twitcher flinched. He was a weedy little man with round shoulders who on most days would not warrant a second glance. He had always suspected that Guy held him in contempt. Now he was certain. He swallowed hard and tried to put on a show of bravado.

"Are you threatening me, Guy?" he asked.

"Yes. Just watch your step or you'll be visiting the dentist. Okay?"

"There's no need to be offensive."

"Offensive? I'd like to know what could be more offensive than spying on your neighbours. Why not install CCTV? That would save you the trouble of hiding behind the curtains."

The twitcher's jaw dropped and left eye blinked rapidly as he sought to control a nervous tic.

"I'm sorry, Guy," he said, "but I shall have to report your comments to the Neighbourhood Watch. Your attitude is totally unacceptable."

"I thought you were the Neighbourhood Watch?"

"I'm a member, certainly, and proud to be one."

"You're not a copper's nark, too, by any chance?"

"What if I am?"

"I'd be absolutely astounded. I thought you were just a snivelling little git who had somehow missed the boat when the Stasi were disbanded."

"The Stasi were before my time," the man said, wiping a trace of spittle from his chin.

"What a pity. You could probably have won the Iron Cross for snooping beyond the call of duty."

Guy noticed that the twitcher had apparently sprung a leak. The front of his trousers displayed the stigma of an involuntary flow and a small puddle began to spread slowly across the pavement. Guy looked at the sky and held out his hand.

"I hadn't realised it was raining," he said.

The snoop belatedly became aware of his plight and flushed deeply. He waited, mute with embarrassment, for Guy to deliver the coup de grâce.

"Just keep your nose out of my business, chum, or you'll be doing more than piss in your pants. Do I make myself clear?"

Turning on his heel, he strode off down the street. The twitcher at last found his voice and cried after him: "By the way, Guy, what was the name of that hotel you stayed at in Cyprus?"

"Plato's Palace," Guy called over his shoulder. "Just ask for Messalina; she'll fix you up."

The rainmaker, humiliated and embarrassed, stood on the pavement for a few moments, uncertain about what to do. He had lost a friend – or at least somebody he liked to think of as a friend -- and wondered how many other people would soon be laughing at his expense. He glanced down at the damp patch on his trousers. With any luck, he could find somewhere to sit in the sun and dry out. He also needed time to think. He was glad he had jotted down the registration number of the ancient Renault that had been parked outside the flat all night. It might well come in handy when he began to plot his revenge.

Chapter XVIII

Guy was still seething with anger when he arrived home. His blood pressure had probably gone through the roof. He should not have allowed the twitcher to provoke him. The man was not worth bothering about. He made himself a pot of coffee and opened the one letter that had arrived while he was out. He was hereby summoned to give evidence at the inquest into the death of Alexei Bukharov, also known as Max Schulman. He tossed it to one side and checked his emails. Nothing of importance there, not even a message from his lady friend whose car had lowered the moral tone of the neighbourhood. He drank his coffee and wondered if the snoop would complain to the landlord or perhaps even report him to the police, claiming he had been threatened with violence. What if he did? He would ensure that the man became even more of a pariah than he already was.

He was about to start work when the telephone once again put off the evil moment. He went into the hall to answer it.

"Hullo?" he said. "Guy Chandler."

There was a slight delay on the line but eventually a far-away voice said: "Guy?"

"Guy speaking."

"Bonjour, mon ami," the caller said. "It's Brother Alphonse. I'm sure you remember me."

"Of course I remember you," Guy assured him, glowing with pleasure. The sound of the priest's voice drove the twitcher from his mind. "How are you – and where are you?"

"I'm fine and at home in France," Brother Alphonse replied. "I thought I'd give you a ring as I may have some information about the missing Corelli."

"Have you, by Jove!" exclaimed Guy. "But let me ring you back. I don't want you to run up a telephone bill on my behalf."

"Don't worry about that," the priest said. "God will provide."

"I'm sure he will. What have you learned?"

"I've just been reading the local newspaper," the priest said, "and noticed an advertisement about an auction of paintings and things in Grenoble. One of the items listed is a picture of a girl with a ceramic urn."

"Do you think it could be *the* girl?" asked Guy.

"I would not like to say. There are probably many paintings of girls with pots of one sort or another. If you like, I'll send you a cut-out and you can make up your own mind."

"Please do," said Guy. "I'd love to see it."

"You'll have to hurry if you wish to attend the sale," the priest warned. "It's only ten days away."

"Okay. As soon as I get the cutting, I'll give you a ring."

Guy returned to his study and drew a deep breath. The brief conversation had dispelled his anger and he felt a lot calmer now. Perhaps that's what the church was for, to apply balm and cool the fevered brow.

The days dragged while Guy waited for the postman to arrive. He tried to concentrate on his novel but words eluded him. Inspiration had been driven out by anticipation of the news from France. Eventually, a small envelope bearing a French stamp dropped through the letterbox. Guy tore it open and scanned the brief note from Brother Alphonse. Then he read the advertisement.

The auctioneers had assembled a large number of artefacts, including paintings, sculptures and various bits and pieces, all of which were to be sold to the highest bidder. They had highlighted some of the more interesting items, including Lot 49, a portrait of a girl with a ceramic urn. Artist unknown. Could this be the picture that Guy – and his late friend Max – had been seeking since the publication of *The Cartesian triangle?* He wouldn't know unless he saw it. That meant a quick trip to France. Even if the exercise plunged him into the red, he could not afford to let the opportunity pass.

The auction was now just four days away. He had no time to lose if he wanted to view the painting before the sale got under way. He checked his bank balance and scrolled through the internet for the cheapest flight to Grenoble. Then he phoned Brother Alphonse.

"I've decided to attend the sale and see the picture for myself," he told the priest. "I won't be able to rest until I do."

"In that case, you must allow me to accompany you. I know Grenoble quite well and can probably save you much travail."

"That's very kind of you but I don't want to put you to any trouble," said Guy.

"No trouble at all," Brother Alphonse replied. "I shall be delighted to show you around."

Guy managed to book a last-minute seat with a small French airline based in Lyon. He planned to arrive the day before the sale, stay overnight, possibly put in a bid if the reserve was low enough and return later the same day. A short visit was essential if costs were to be kept down. Grenoble was not exactly the cheapest place in the world. He phoned the priest to let him know when he would be arriving. They agreed to meet at the Café Mistral which Brother Alphonse assured him was close to the saleroom.

A couple of days later, Guy packed an overnight bag and set off for France. The plane touched down at Lyon, where most of the passengers got off. How many were coppers heading for Interpol, he wondered. At least Miss Kovalski was not among them. After a brief stop, the aircraft flew on to Grenoble, a few miles to the south. Guy took the bus into the city and enquired the whereabouts of the Café Mistral. He found it easily enough and, clutching his bag, ventured inside. He hoped he didn't look too much like a tourist.

The place was crowded and at first he did not recognise the priest. The man of god had dispensed with his cassock and was wearing a sports jacket and an open-necked shirt. He looked even more like a rugby player than when they had first met in Figueras.

"Hullo, my friend," the monk said, smiling broadly. "As you can see, I'm on sabbatical, for 24 hours, at least."

"I hope the bishop has given his blessing," said Guy.

The Benedictine shrugged. "What the eye doesn't see..."

They ordered coffee and, after catching up on events since their return from Montserrat, made their way down the street towards the saleroom, an ancient building that had survived innumerable conflicts. Brother Alphonse pushed open the door and they went inside. Like most auction rooms, except those where the rich gathered to flaunt their wealth, the place exuded a slightly musty smell. The odour was distinctly French, however, redolent of cowhide, garlic and old wine, with a hint of dry rot and ancient cigar smoke. Guy surmised that many items must have come from dusty attics or storerooms deep in the country. Even to his unsophisticated eye, the goods were never going to make the grade at Sotheby's. Artistic junk of every description, from winged angels to the occasional piece of erotica, filled the entire ground floor. The paintings were gathered in one corner.

"Here we are," said Brother Alphonse, casting an appreciative eye over them. "The end of the rainbow."

"All we need now is a pot of gold," Guy remarked.

"Preferably two pots," the priest said. "The church can always find a use for one."

Turning to his companion, he whispered: "Try not to appear too keen. The saleroom has one thousand eyes and, if you look interested in anything, you'll end up bidding against yourself."

"I understand," Guy replied quietly, "although I doubt if I could afford to buy much, anyway."

Half a dozen other people, most of them men, poked around, occasionally making a note of something that might be worth buying. Bargain-hunters or possibly dealers calculating the amount of profit they would make when the goods were tarted up and re-sold in some trendy boutique or gallery. Guy wondered if the new price would include woodworm.

"That's very odd," he said, as they searched for the picture described in the advertisement. "Lot 49 seems to be missing."

"It must be somewhere," the monk replied, sounding not overly confident. "Unless it has been put on display by itself."

While they hunted among the bric-a-brac for a girl with an earthenware jar, a man in a dustcoat came along, carrying a small statuette.

"Excuse me," the priest said, speaking in French. "Lot 49, I don't see it anywhere."

The man put down the statuette, probably a late entry, and consulted his catalogue.

"Lot 49," he said. "Withdrawn from sale."

"Withdrawn from sale?" the priest gasped.

"Sold prior to auction," the usher confirmed, putting the catalogue back in his pocket.

"But this gentleman has come all the way from England to see it," Brother Alphonse exclaimed, forgetting his own advice to Guy a few moments earlier not to appear too keen.

"I'm sorry, Monsieur. But somebody made an offer a few days ago. It was accepted by the vendor and the buyer called in yesterday to collect it."

Guy was listening intently and judged the tenor of the conversation by the look of dismay on the priest's face.

"Who was the buyer? " the monk asked. "Do you know?"

"A woman from your friend's part of the world," the man replied. "That is all I am permitted to say."

"But, surely, you can tell me who the vendor was?"

"As I recall, the painting formed part of the estate of somebody who died several years ago. The trustees must have got tired of waiting for a buyer and decided to put it under the hammer. I don't think it was worth much, anyway. Now, if you'll excuse me, Monsieur, I must get on. The sale starts promptly at ten o'clock tomorrow morning."

Brother Alphonse turned to Guy and said gloomily: "I am so sorry, my friend. The painting has been withdrawn. I have brought you all this way on a wild duck chase."

"You have done nothing of the kind," said Guy, placing a comforting hand on the priest's arm. "It was my decision to come to France and you must not feel guilty."

"But I do," the priest declared.

"That's because you are burdened with the woes of the world," said Guy. "How was anybody to know the painting would be sold before it could be auctioned?"

"I should have guessed."

For the first time, they noticed a man standing nearby, ostensibly looking at the items on display. He was well-dressed in a Bohemian sort of way, but not flashily so. He glanced casually at the paintings but seemed more interested in the frames than in the pictures themselves. He looked up and caught their eye.

"Forgive me, Messieurs," he said, "but I could not help overhearing your conversation. I, too, have had a wasted journey."

Brother Alphonse recognised the man's accent and spoke to him in German. It was not a language that had left its mark on Guy. After a brief chat, the stranger moved on.

"Who was that?" Guy asked.

"A painter, originally from the Democratic Republic. He now lives in Switzerland, apparently."

"What was his name?"

"He didn't say. But the painting – the auctioneers' description of it, anyway – reminded him of one he had seen many years ago on a trip to France."

"Did he say who the artist was?"

"No. He'd probably forgotten."

Guy thought it odd that the man could remember the painting but not the artist, especially as he was a painter himself. But it would have been churlish to press the matter.

The priest looked sadly at the author. His pursuit of the missing Corelli had led them both down yet another blind alley.

"I don't know how to apologise, Guy," he said. "You have come all this way for nothing. You must let me take you out to dinner to make up for it."

"Stop worrying, father," said Guy, aware that most priests could barely afford to feed themselves, let alone strangers. "It's not your fault. Relax. Forget about it."

"I wish I could."

"I'm sure that if you said three Hail Marys and promised to give yourself a good thrashing you'd feel a lot better."

Brother Alphonse chuckled.

"I shall arrange for the Sisters of Charity to scourge me," he said. "As it happens, I am staying with one tonight."

"Lucky old you. Van Gogh had to scourge himself."

"Van Gogh?"

"He was a priest, or at least a pastor, before he took up painting."

"No wonder he went mad," Brother Alphonse remarked. "The pulpit and the palette. A fatal mix."

Guy decided it was time to find his hotel. He might just as well stay the night now he was here and attend the sale in the morning. After a cursory glance at the other paintings and objets d'art, none of which grabbed his attention, he shouldered his bag and prepared to kick his heels for a few hours. The girl with the earthenware jar had given him the slip once again.

"I wonder," he said as they left the auction room, "if the buyer could have been a member of the Schulman family?"

"The Schulman family?"

The priest seemed startled by the suggestion.

"They weren't all wiped out," said Guy, recalling his conversation with Max. "Several survived the war and are said to be quite rich again. They probably have agents all over Europe, keeping an eye out for property they once owned."

Brother Alphonse was clearly taken aback and struggled to maintain his composure.

"Why would they buy a painting that was already theirs?" he asked. "They would simply demand that the seller hand it over or they would take him to court."

"Maybe they figured it wasn't worth the hassle," Guy replied. "It would be cheaper just to buy it. The price tends to go up once lawyers are involved."

"That's true."

As they walked down the street, Brother Alphonse appeared lost in thought, oblivious even to the admiring glances of passing women. Suddenly he seemed to remember something.

"Excuse me for one moment," he said, taking his mobile phone from his jacket. "I must make a quick phone call."

He dialled a number and exchanged a few words in what sounded like Russian with whoever answered. Then he put the phone back in his pocket.

"Sorry about that," he said. "Come on. I think we could do with a drink."

A drink: that's what they needed to restore their spirits. Plus some food. Guy hadn't eaten since breakfast in Blackheath. He was more than peckish.

Brother Alphonse led the way unerringly through the side streets to a small bistro tucked away in a courtyard. For a man of the cloth, he was remarkably familiar with the watering holes of Grenoble.

"You seem to know your way around pretty well," Guy said with admiration.

"The legacy of a misspent youth," the priest acknowledged.

That was clear the moment they entered the bistro. The patron smiled as he recognised Brother Alphonse and shook his hand warmly.

"Hullo, father," he beamed. Noting the priest's casual attire, he added: "You've not abandoned your calling, I hope?"

"A break from routine, that's all. There are still enough sinners to keep me in business – I'm glad to say."

He introduced Guy and they took a seat at one of the small tables. A delicious aroma – redolent of ham, herbs, olives and brie -- emanated from the kitchen, sharpening their appetite. Guy ordered a bottle of Burgundy, some soup and French bread and pâté. As they waited to be served, several people approached the table to say hello. Brother Alphonse was obviously not only well-known but very popular.

"Will you be staying for the sale?" he asked as the food arrived.

"I might as well," said Guy. "My flight doesn't leave until tomorrow and I've already booked my hotel. What about you?"

"I must be back in Briançon in time for mass," the priest replied. "I will catch the early bus."

"Provided your sister remembers to wake you up in time."

"I probably won't get much sleep, anyway."

They fell silent for a moment or two, relishing their food. The priest ate ravenously, pausing only to sip his wine. Their failure to find the painting was obviously weighing on his mind.

"I wonder," he said, "if we could be dealing with a case of mistaken identity?"

"Mistaken identity? In what way?"

"Well," said Brother Alphonse, spreading a generous helping of pâté on to his bread, "some years ago a painting by Caravaggio was discovered in the attic of a farmhouse near Toulouse."

"Toulouse? That's a long way from Grenoble."

"Maybe, but the circumstances are very similar. It's possible that the people looking for Corelli's *Girl with terracotta pot* may have confused the two."

"Possible, but unlikely."

"It wouldn't be the first time that treasure hunters had followed a false trail," said Brother Alphonse.

"Treasure hunters?"

"The Caravaggio is worth a great deal of money. That always clouds people's judgement."

Guy took a mouthful of wine and considered the matter. A coincidence, yes, but not one that bore much scrutiny. For a start, the Italian had been born in Milan four hundred years earlier and his style was too well known for there to be any confusion. His pictures were dark and sombre and invariably had a biblical theme. Corelli's radiated warmth and sunshine, reflecting his years in Africa. Besides, the *Girl with terracotta pot* came from a Jewish family in Vienna, not a farmhouse in Toulouse, and had yet to be discovered anywhere.

"An interesting theory," he said, "but their styles are totally different. I'm sure nobody would ever confuse the two – or three, if you count my *Girl with the earthenware jar*."

"I thought I'd mention it, all the same."

"What's the Caravaggio about?" asked Guy.

"Murder," the priest replied. "It shows Judith, a widow from Bethulia, killing Holofernes."

"Who was Holofernes?"

"A Syrian warlord. The bitch seduced him, then cut off his head while he slept."

"I hope it won't give your sister ideas. I should hate you to end up like Mr Bobbitt."

"Mr Bobbitt?"

"An American gentleman whose wife operated on him without his consent."

"Oh, yes, I remember!" the priest laughed. "Caravaggio was a bit of a wild man himself, you know. He killed somebody, then had to spend the rest of his life on the run."

"I hope he didn't come to a sticky end."

"His death was rather tragic, as it happens. Some of the paint he used got into his bloodstream and he died of lead poisoning."

Guy recalled that his friend Max had also died of lead poisoning. His blood had stopped circulating, thanks to a Russian bullet.

They chatted idly for a while, enjoying their wine and absorbing the atmosphere of the bistro. Brother Alphonse revealed that he had spent some time in Rome, learning the ropes as a very junior cleric at the Vatican.

"Is that where you picked up your knowledge of the art world?" Guy asked.

"I picked up a lot of things in Rome," the priest laughed.

Guy suspected that his companion, with his good looks and easy manner, was destined for higher things. Briançon was probably the first step on the clerical ladder. One day, perhaps, Brother Alphonse might be recalled to Rome to help the Vatican impose a little discipline, especially in financial matters. After all the scandals of recent years, the Catholic church needed somebody who could deliver a firm smack of authority. The Holy Father himself still had questions to answer about his links to the military junta in Argentina.

They squeezed the last drop from the bottle and prepared reluctantly to leave. Guy walked over to the cash desk to pay. The patron shook his head.

"Any friend of Brother Alphonse is a friend of mine," he said. "You are my guest."

Guy tried to insist on payment but the patron would have none of it. Guy was embarrassed and wondered if the priest knew they would not be charged. After another attempt to pay, he conceded defeat and shook the man's hand.

"I am most obliged," he said.

"You're welcome," the bar keeper replied.

The shadows were lengthening as they left the bistro and walked down the street. Guy was shocked to discover how much time they had spent there, lingering over their wine. He had not yet checked into his hotel.

"Where are you staying?" the priest asked.

Guy named a small hotel where he had managed to book a room over the internet.

"You must let me show you the way," the priest said. "It's not far."

Once again, Brother Alphonse proved that he knew Grenoble like the back of his hand and within a few minute they arrived at the hotel.

"You have chosen well," he said. "I have stayed here myself."

Guy thanked the priest for his help and said goodbye. He was truly sorry to see the man of god depart. They had got on well, surprisingly so in view of his professed atheism. Brother Alphonse had proved to be catholic in the true sense of the word, with a wide range of interests and a deep understanding of human nature. He hoped they would meet again.

He checked in and was shown to his room, a large and comfortable chamber on the first floor. After half a bottle of Burgundy, he found it hard to stay awake. As he turned out the light and fell into bed, he just hoped the drains were in good working order.

Shortly before ten the following morning, after breakfasting on coffee and croissants, he made his way back to the saleroom. He wanted to see who was there, even if Lot 49 wasn't. Of the painter from Switzerland, there was no sign. Perhaps, like Guy, he had abandoned all hope of seeing the painting again. The auctioneer rattled through the catalogue, barely pausing for breath, and jumped straight from Lot 48 to Lot 50, a landscape of a garden in Provence. Neither picture attracted much interest and were knocked down at virtually give-away prices. Somebody would probably make a nice profit.

Swallowing his disappointment, Guy headed for the airport to catch the plane home. His efforts to solve the mystery of the girl with the earthenware jar seemed destined to end in failure.

Chapter XIX

A wasted journey? Possibly. Guy had nothing to show for it, except a hole in his bank account. But experience was never wasted, he told himself, however futile it appeared at the time. He had lost only a day or two and had learned something about Caravaggio, a wild man with a criminal record whose paintings fetched millions. He'd also had the pleasure of meeting Brother Alphonse again. Without the priest to guide him, he really would have wasted a lot of time in Grenoble.

As he contemplated his next move, Guy wondered idly what had become of Miss Kovalski. It was she, after all, who had set the ball rolling by turning up at the launch of *The Cartesian triangle*. But, as one event followed another, the image of an attractive young woman interested in books had been overtaken by reality. Perhaps it was just as well that, if she really were a copper, she no longer dominated his thoughts.

Uppermost in his mind at present was the need to restore his finances. The trip to Grenoble may have been short but it was also costly. And his next royalty cheque, if indeed there were to be one after the publisher had deducted his advance, was still a couple of months away. It looked like another stint at Crosbie, Grimshaw and Snape. Not that he minded. The agency paid well and he enjoyed putting his mind to work on a marketing problem. He just wished that he could earn as much by writing novels.

One morning, as he was grappling with the plot, the doorbell rang. Irked by the interruption, Guy went to the door to see who was impeding the flow of literature. He was startled to find a police officer in uniform standing there.

"Mr Chandler?" the copper enquired.

"Yes," Guy replied, hesitantly. For a moment, he wondered if the creep across the foyer had lodged a formal complaint.

"I wonder if I could have a word with you, sir?"

Guy invited the plod to step inside and take a seat. It was the second time the police had arrived at his flat within the space of a few months. Any more and the neighbours would begin to talk.

The plod, a burly man with a poker face, sat down and placed his helmet on the settee. It was hard to tell from his expression whether this was a friendly visit or not.

"How can I help?" asked Guy, relieved that the man was only a constable. Trouble usually arrived with those of higher rank.

"I've been instructed by the coroner to enquire why you did not attend the inquest into the death of the man known as Max Schulman," the plod said.

Guy felt as though he had been struck with a hammer. He had completely forgotten about the inquest.

"Did you not receive the letter summoning you to attend?"

Guy got up and went into the study. His head swam as he rummaged among the papers on his desk until he found the summons.

"Yes, I did receive it," he admitted, somewhat superfluously. "But I've been so busy lately that I forgot all about it."

"We are all very busy, sir," the copper said, "but a summons is a summons. The coroner is not very pleased."

"I don't suppose he is."

"He was going to have you arrested for contempt of court."

"Oh, lord."

"Fortunately, he concluded that your evidence was unlikely to help him establish the cause of death."

"Thank god for that," said Guy. He looked at the date set for the inquest. "As it happens, I was out of the country on that day."

"That's no excuse," the copper said. "You ought to have informed the coroner."

"I shall write and apologise without delay," said Guy.

"I strongly advise you to do so."

"What was the verdict, by the way?"

"Murder, by person or persons unknown."

"I suppose that means a murder enquiry?"

"Of course. It has already begun."

"Well, I hope you don't intend to interrogate me again," said

Guy. "I only met the blighter once and have no idea how my telephone number came to be in his wallet."

"I think I can say that you are probably in the clear, sir. But may I suggest that you read your mail more carefully in future?"

"I certainly shall," said Guy.

The copper stood up and prepared to leave. As Guy accompanied him to the door, the plod asked: "Incidentally, where did you go?"

"France," said Guy.

"Not Cyprus this time?"

"Cyprus?" said Guy, catching his breath. "I've never been to Cyprus in my life."

A ripple of surprise flickered across the plod's impassive features. Maybe he wouldn't make such a good poker player, after all. Guy wondered how much other information the police held on their data base about him.

He showed the copper out and breathed a sigh of relief. He had been let off with a caution. Next time, if there were to be a next time, he might not be so lucky. But at least he now had proof that the incontinent wretch across the foyer was not only snooping on his neighbours but snitching on them, too. The reference to Cyprus left him in no doubt. Despite his anger, Guy could not help laughing. The copper had inadvertently shot the nark in the foot. A casual remark, no more than a slip of the tongue, had undermined his credibility. The fuzz would think twice about believing him in future.

Chapter XX

The inhabitants of Klugersdorf were not, on the whole, an inquisitive lot. They liked to know what was going on, of course, but were disinclined to pry into their neighbours' affairs. What their fellow citizens did in their own homes was none of their business. Everybody had the right to privacy, whether enshrined in law or not. They did like to gossip, however, and it was with some relish that they began to speculate on the disappearance of Herr Neuberger, the painter who lived at the top end of the village.

Herr Neuberger had not been seen for some time. The German was hardly the most gregarious of souls but could usually be relied on to stop and pass the time of day on those rare occasions he ventured out. Moreover, the butcher, the baker and the purveyor of fresh fruit and vegetables had come to expect a call at least once a week when he phoned to place an order. But for almost a month now they had not heard from him. Even the lights of the chalet were not turned on when the sun set in the evening. Either he was on a diet, on holiday or something was wrong.

There was much talk about his car, the expensive saloon that had been parked in his driveway for many a moon and which had aroused feelings of envy. One morning, a couple of weeks after Herr Neuberger himself had disappeared, the villagers awoke to discover it was no longer there. It had been driven away, stealthily and without fanfare, in the night. That in itself may not have been significant were it not for the fact that the painter himself was still missing.

The leading citizens of Klugersdorf convened a meeting to discuss the situation. They were not – they tried to convince themselves -- being sticky-beaks, just good neighbours. They would not like to think they had stood by and done nothing while one of their number was in distress. After careful consideration, it was decided that two or three folk who knew Herr Neuberger better than most should call at the chalet to check that all was well. It would be regrettable, a slap in the face almost, if after all these years their resident artist had simply upped sticks and sought pastures new without telling anybody.

The delegation, if one could call it that, assembled at the mayor's house to discuss strategy. How would they explain their visit? A friendly call to express their concern, a polite enquiry to see if he needed anything? Bread, milk, potatoes? As good neighbours, they would be happy to deliver whatever he wanted. Any suggestion that they were seeking an excuse to invade his privacy must be avoided at all costs. The three men – it had been thought advisable to exclude women in case Herr Neuberger was found to be found in a state of déshabillé, or worse – made their way warily up the main street to the German's chalet and rang the bell.

"What shall we say if he's got a woman in there?" asked the barber, an elderly man who knew more about his fellow citizens than most.

"That would be better than finding a boy," the tavern keeper replied.

"We'll play it by ear," the mayor decreed. "Let him make the first move."

A cold wind blew from the mountains as they waited on the patio for Herr Neuberger to open the door. Autumn had arrived and the first snow of winter could not be far off. In a week or two, the village would again be cut off from the outside world. The tavern keeper cast his eye towards the garage where the German's car, the object of such envy, had been parked.

"It's curious that the car is missing," he said. "Herr Neuberger couldn't drive, as far as I know."

"It wasn't doing much good, just sitting there," the mayor replied. "Maybe he's sold it. It must be worth a few pfennigs."

The mayor gave the front door, a wooden structure worthy of a small castle, a tentative shove. It refused to budge. He rang the bell again.

"We can't stand here all day," said the barber, shuffling nervously and shivering in the cold air. "What shall we do?"

“Let's have a peep through the window,” the mayor suggested. “If he's there, we'll soon know.”

As usual, the curtains of the room facing the street were drawn to prevent passers-by observing the artist at work. Undaunted, the mayor led the well-intentioned Samaritans down the path at the side of the house until they found a window that offered a view of the interior. Putting his nose to the glass, he peeped inside. He drew back in shock. The scene that met his eye was one of devastation. Furniture had been overturned, papers and paint scattered. It was clear that the house had been ransacked.

“My god!” he gasped. “We must call the police.”

That such a wanton act of vandalism had occurred on his patch appalled him. Klugersdorf was proud of its reputation as a place where crime was virtually unheard of. Anything that impugned its status as an island of tranquillity would be disastrous. The last thing the villagers wanted was the arrival of a horde of journalists asking embarrassing questions. Publicity must be avoided at all costs. The situation nevertheless demanded action. The barber switched on his mobile phone and hurriedly dialled the emergency number. When the police answered, he blurted out the facts as they were known. He was instructed to remain where he was and not allow anyone to enter the property.

Klugersdorf was a small village, too small to warrant a gendarmerie of its own. It would take at least half an hour for the police to travel from their base further down the valley. Despite the instruction to stay where they were, the three men decided it would be warmer and more comfortable to wait at home than stand outside in the cold. They walked back to the mayor's house and waited for the constabulary to arrive.

Half an hour or so later, a police car drove slowly down the main street, its occupants looking for signs of disorder. The mayor ran out, waving his arms.

“Follow me,” he ordered the two gendarmes in the vehicle.

The mayor strode self-importantly towards the German's house, followed by his companions and several villagers who realised that something must be wrong. A police car in Klugersdorf! Such an event was not to be missed. Nothing quite like it had been seen in their Alpine retreat since a visiting statesman had been killed by an avalanche many years ago.

The mayor ordered the driver to pull up by the gate and led the two men down the side of the house to the vantage point. One of them peered through the window and sucked in a lungful of cold air. The long drive up the valley had not been in vain. Calling up his superiors on the radio, he reported his findings. Then he ordered the mayor and the villagers off the property.

"This a potential crime scene and I must instruct you to keep away," he said as the mayor bristled with indignation. This was his village and nobody told him what to do.

The delegation, followed by a growing crowd of onlookers, returned to the mayor's house. The villagers babbled excitedly, wondering what could possibly have happened to Herr Neuberger. The last person known to have seen him, a farmer on the way to feed his cows, recalled the encounter. The German had exchanged greetings but had been as taciturn as ever. The baker observed that Herr Neuberger had recently changed his order for pastries, preferring those with reduced fat. The man who mowed the grass and pruned the roses remarked casually that he had not been paid. But otherwise there was nothing to suggest that the artist was in trouble or the victim of crime. Perhaps he had simply grown tired of his rustic existence and had decided to see what the big, bad world beyond the Alps could offer.

Within twenty minutes or so, two more police cars swept into the village and screeched to a halt outside the German's house. Half a dozen officers jumped out and joined their colleagues in the garden. After a brief discussion, one of them returned to his car, rummaged among the box of house-breaking equipment on the back seat and selected a small bunch of keys. It took only a few seconds for him to find the right one and open the front door. Four of the men went inside, leaving the others to form a cordon and prevent busybodies from gaining access.

The scene inside the house was much as the mayor had described. Tables and chairs had been overturned, possessions scattered. One or two plates had been broken, possibly by sliding off the table, but actual damage was slight. The fridge was still working, as was the freezer. Neither contained much food. The police hunted in vain for a computer but Herr Neuberger was apparently able to survive without one. The one letter in the mail box proved to be a circular from an investment company. At this stage, it was impossible to say whether anything had been stolen. A quick search revealed no sign of a body. That was a relief but did not rule out foul play. Moreover, it was entirely feasible that the owner might walk through the door at any moment and demand to know what the hell they were doing in his house.

The officer in charge stood back and surveyed the scene. To his experienced eye, the damage suggested a gratuitous act of vandalism – by a woman, perhaps – rather than wanton destruction. A man would have trashed the place with more vigour. Whoever it was, the culprit clearly had access to the house. The motive was not so clear.

"I suppose we'll have to call in the forensic boys," he said. "In the meantime, you had better cordon off the place."

"What about the villagers, chief?" asked one of his men.

"Pull in a few of them for questioning," the chief replied, "starting with whoever made the phone call."

The investigation quickly ran out of steam. The police questioned half a dozen villagers but nobody seemed to know anything about the artist. To most inhabitants, Herr Neuberger was a man of mystery. They knew only that he was a painter who had lived among them for many years. Had he gone mad, like Van Gogh, and destroyed his own work before heading for the hills and committing suicide? There was nothing to suggest that he might have taken his own life.

The police might have expected to find more paintings in the house. There was not even much work in progress. A few sketches of various subjects but nothing that caused them to think he was about to embark on a major project. There were, however, a number of books, including a novel by an English writer. Herr Neuberger would not be the first German to read a novel in English, of course, but the book seemed to be out of place among all the German and French literature.

The forensic team, wearing rubber gloves, went over the house, inch by inch. Their efforts were hampered by the fact that they did not know what they were supposed to be looking for. They were not even sure that a crime had been committed. Clues were few and far between. There was no trace of blood and a couple of broken plates did not point to either kidnap or murder. The criminal investigation branch examined a handful of bank statements they found in the bedroom but were frustrated when the bank refused to hand over details of the German's account. Despite its reluctant move towards more transparency, Switzerland was still a place where the innocent could rely on a degree of privacy. If the police could provide evidence that the artist had been involved in money laundering or other illegal activity, the bank would have to cooperate. But until then it was none of their business what Herr Neuberger did with his money.

The manager in Bern recalled, however, that he had recently questioned Herr Neuberger about his decision to pay funds into an account in Malta. At the time, there was no reason to think that the German was acting illegally. It was his money and, provided he remained within the law, he could do what he liked with it. But three weeks ago, Herr Neuberger had transferred a large amount of money to the island. The manager pored over the details but could see nothing to warrant further investigation. Since then, no money had been withdrawn and the account remained in credit, healthily so.

After several days of fruitless activity, the police concluded that Herr Neuberger was probably the victim of an emotional bust-up and that the little lady had vented her anger by wrecking the joint. But unless the householder complained there was nothing they could do. They were not marriage counsellors. That might be how the British police saw their role but it wasn't the Swiss way of doing things. If they were called out to settle every domestic argument, they would never have time to track down drug smugglers and illegal immigrants.

They locked up the house and went away, marking the file 'No further action'.

The villagers of Klugersdorf relaxed and went about their business. They fitted the wooden shutters, checked the central heating, stacked the logs outside the kitchen door and prepared for winter. Herr Neuberger would no doubt return in due course and life would go on as usual. For the time being, they had other things to worry about.

Chapter XXI

In Blackheath, too, the days grew shorter. The office girls put away (in many cases, threw away) their summer clothes while the massed ranks of commuters searched their wardrobes for something warmer. In the park, the squirrels scurried back and forth, storing whatever food they could find for the winter. The leaves changed colour and fell to the ground, clogging gutters and blocking drains. The last of the summer flowers withered and died. So far, the capital had been spared the cold winds from the east but sooner or later they were bound to arrive. When they did, life would not be so pleasant. Until then, Guy was happy to make the journey twice a week to the offices of Crosbie, Grimshaw and Snape in the West End where he busied himself on a number of accounts. It was far more enjoyable to work there than huddle over his computer at home, waiting for the landlord to turn on the heating. Besides, he could always find an excuse to drop into the art director's studio and chat about Corelli.

"My religious friend thinks it might be a case of mistaken identity," he said.

"I doubt it," Grant replied. "Caravaggio had talent. Corelli didn't. Not much, anyway. Besides, his work fetches millions. I can't see Corelli ever setting the art market on fire."

"Maybe some people think he will."

"Hope springs eternal," said Grant.

One evening, after a hard day striving to produce an ad. that would satisfy a particularly fastidious client, Guy returned home exhausted. He could see why the agency had pushed the account in his direction. Everybody else thought the man was a complete anorak, devoid of both wit and humour, and tried to avoid him. How he had ever been appointed to the post of marketing manager was a mystery. He would have been more at home as a deck-chair attendant. For the sake of a guaranteed income on at least two days a week, Guy was prepared to put up with him.

He drew the curtains, opened a can of soup – not quite up to the standard of that in Grenoble – and checked the telephone for messages. There was just one: from Mandy, asking him to call. She sounded agitated. She was not the hysterical type, so something must have upset her. He had not heard from her since their night of love. He hoped she wasn't pregnant. After he had eaten he returned her call.

"What's the problem?" he asked when she answered the phone.

"Oh, Guy, darling. I've had a horrible letter."

"A letter? Who from?"

"Your neighbour. He's trying to blackmail me."

For a moment, Guy was speechless. Blackmail was not a word that boded well for a relaxed evening.

"You mean the little shit across the hall?" he asked.

"I guess so. It's from your address."

"What does he say?"

"You'd better read it yourself," replied Mandy. "Do you want to come round?"

"It would be quicker if you came here."

"Okay. Give me half an hour."

Guy was about to hang up when he remembered the twitcher's habits.

"Don't park outside the flat," he warned. "And don't ring the bell. I'll leave the door on the latch."

Guy wished he had something stronger than coffee in the house. He needed a drink to steady his nerves. But alcohol and the creative process didn't mix, whatever Hemingway might have said. He was also angry with himself for asking Mandy not to park outside the flat. He recalled Tanya's words: "You're not afraid of a pathetic little snoop, are you?" No, he wasn't. But on this occasion he had succumbed a mild dose of paranoia.

He did not hear his visitor arrive and was surprised when she slipped into the room and put her arms around him.

"Long time, no see," she said. "I thought you must have forgotten me."

"I'm not that gaga," he replied, noting how worried she looked.

"I didn't phone in case your husband was at home."

"No chance of that. He's way up in Lapland or some such place."

"Helping Father Christmas to fill a few stockings, no doubt?"

"Mrs Christmas, more likely."

He returned her embrace and they exchanged an affectionate kiss. He resisted the urge to drag her into the bedroom and make love.

"What has that obnoxious little man been saying?" he asked.

Mandy took the letter from her bag and gave it to him. It comprised a single page, scrawled in Biro on lined paper. Guy read it quickly and gritted his teeth. Then he began to chuckle.

"I don't see what's so funny," she said. "What if he tells Chris I spent the night here?"

"He won't," said Guy, reading the letter again.

"You sound very confident."

"I am."

The snoop was not exactly subtle. He had obviously been reading too many stories about the KGB and the methods it had used to blackmail people. They were experts; the snoop was not. It was clear from the very first line that he was a bungling amateur. He could barely spell his name, let alone threaten a happily-married woman. The gist of the letter was that he knew she had stayed at the flat overnight and might be inclined to tell her husband, unless she met his conditions. What were those conditions? Hush money? A carnal encounter? He was not specific. Perhaps he was too scared to spell them out.

"What a creep," said Guy. "I doubt if he could mount a photo in a frame, let alone a lady on all fours."

"Do you think I ought to notify the police?"

"Not unless you wish your husband to know what you get up to while he's at sea."

"He has a pretty good idea already."

"Don't worry, my sweet. We'll call his bluff."

"How?" asked Mandy.

"Leave it to me."

He noticed she was wearing jeans, probably the same ones that had helped to arouse his desire when they first met at the Meridian Club. Expensive and stylish, they were designed to flatter the body and conceal the flaws.

"Would you like to stay the night?" he asked.

"I'd love to but it's the wrong time of the month, I'm afraid."

"Just my luck."

"In any case, I've arranged to call on Tanya."

"Tanya?"

"You haven't forgotten her as well?"

"Hardly."

"We have book-club business to discuss."

"So long as you don't discuss any other business."

"I can't promise," Amanda teased. "You know what we girls are like."

"I'm still taking lessons," said Guy.

They exchanged another kiss, more sensual this time, and his hands wandered over her breasts. She seemed a lot calmer now, reassured by his dismissal of the threat.

"You'd better not keep her waiting," he said, reluctantly setting her free. "Leave the letter with me and I'll be in touch."

As she was leaving, Mandy said: "There's one thing I don't understand. How did he find my address?"

"Quite easily, I imagine. He probably circulated your numberplate among his friends in the Neighbourhood Watch and asked them to keep an eye open. He could even have called in a favour from the fuzz."

"The police? They wouldn't tell him where I lived, would they?"

"The police will do anything if you make it worth their while," said Guy.

When she had gone, he sat down and read the letter again. This blatant attempt at extortion was so ludicrous that Guy wondered whether it was supposed to be taken seriously. The KGB had usually backed up their threats with photographic evidence, some of it quite explicit. The snoop offered no more than a few vague observations. A car parked in the street overnight was not proof of an extra-marital affaire. It might simply have broken down. The letter was also full of grammatical errors and spelling mistakes. They alone offended Guy's sense of propriety. He put the missive to one side and began to compose a response. It was a welcome diversion from his labours with the book.

The twitcher, still smarting from his encounter with Guy, had made himself scarce. There was no sign of him in the foyer or even behind the curtains. He had obviously decided to keep out of harm's way. His teeth were the only ones he had.

The best way to deal with the threat, Guy decided, was to take it at face value while at the same time exposing the snoop to ridicule. The man needed to be given a taste of his own medicine. A spoonful of satire might help it to stick in his gullet. After working on his response for a couple of days, Guy phoned Mandy and arranged to meet her at The Coffee Shop. She was already there when he arrived. He was glad she had found a table at the back of the café. Discretion was the order of the day.

"Hullo," she said, hiding her pleasure behind a bland smile.

They shook hands formally, avoiding any hint of intimacy. One never knew who might be watching. Big Brother paled into insignificance alongside the legions of Little Sisters willing to spy on their neighbours. This is what life must have been like under the Stasi. Constant surveillance that stymied any spontaneous act of emotion. Guy could not understand why so many people were apparently quite happy to go along with it. If it was wrong for Germany, it was wrong for Britain.

He ordered a cappuccino for Mandy and a double espresso for himself.

"What have you got to show me?" asked Mandy after the waitress had gone.

"For the time being, just a letter," Guy replied, taking a sheet of paper from his pocket.

"Have a read," he said, unfolding it and passing it across the table.

The letter was neatly typed on headed paper. He sat back while she ran her eye over it and then waited for her to read it properly.

Godiva Escort Agency

(incorporating Pussy Calor)

Dear Mr Wormald,

Thank you for your letter addressed to Mrs Scott-Hopkins. I regret to say that our girls are not permitted to communicate directly with clients. Your letter has therefore has been passed to me for reply.

Mandy looked up and said: "I didn't pass it on. Did you?

"I hope you don't mind?" said Guy, amused and gratified that his efforts had already passed muster.

Mandy frowned and continued reading.

I should like to thank you for your enquiry and have pleasure in providing a brief outline of our services. A member of our sales team will call on you shortly to discuss your requirements in detail.

Godiva Escort Agency is the country's leading supplier of Pussy for Pleasure. Our clients are drawn from across the social spectrum and include hedonists from all walks of life. Many are household names.

The girls are recruited only from the best families

and are well-versed in the vagaries of human nature. They have unrivalled experience of conditions such as impotence, premature ejaculation and all forms of incontinence. Nothing is likely to discomfit them and you may be assured of their discretion.

Godiva escorts are checked regularly by qualified medical practitioners based in Harley Street to ensure they are able to exercise their profession without risk to themselves or their clients.

"This outfit sounds like a cross between a VD clinic and a brothel," said Mandy, looking puzzled. "I can't imagine any really nice girl wanting to work there.

"Can't you?" said Guy, sipping his coffee.

Before enrolling you as a member of this exclusive club, however, we shall require a number of references, including a doctor's certificate confirming that you are free from any form of sexually-transmitted disease, including HIV, and are not a carrier of tuberculosis or swine fever.

We shall also need your permission to undertake an enhanced CRB check. This is to protect our girls from the dangers inherent in the escort business. As you will appreciate, the health and safety of our employees is of paramount importance. For this reason, they are not allowed to offer S&M, bondage or anything that may involve physical pain or violence.

Please note that our terms and conditions do not include refreshment. Our ladies will expect to be wined and dined in a manner commensurate with their status. They can either entertain you at home or meet you at one of the hotels with which we have negotiated a special deal for overnight stays (bed and breakfast only).

Repeat bookings *must* be made through the agency and not negotiated with the girls themselves. Any breach of this rule will result in the immediate cancellation of your membership.

Thank you once again for your enquiry. I look forward to receiving details of your bank account, general health and criminal record so that your application for membership may proceed.

In the meantime, please address any correspondence to me, and not to Mrs Scott-Hopkins.

Yours faithfully,
Lulu Sanchez

Mandy finished reading the letter and her frown deepened. She looked baffled.

"Who is Lulu Sanchez?" she asked.

"Your boss," said Guy.

"But I don't know anybody named Lulu Sanchez."

"Listen, dummkopf," said Guy, sighing with exasperation. "I've spent a whole day writing this letter and all you can do is ask who Lulu is."

Mandy bit her lip and began to read the letter again. Gradually, her frown gave way to a smile and then a chuckle. Suddenly she was convulsed with laughter.

"Gosh! I'm stupid," she said, as people at nearby tables turned to look at her. Guy hoped that none of the ladies from the Meridian Club were enjoying a morning coffee. He did not want their tryst to be reported back to Tanya.

"Oh, this is wonderful!" exclaimed Mandy, now smiling broadly. "What are you going to do with it?"

"What do you think I'm going to do with it? Send it to him, of course."

"But you can't do that!"

"Why not? The man's a complete arsehole. He's trying to blackmail you and needs to be taught a lesson."

"But suppose. . ."

"Suppose nothing," said Guy. "I'll print another copy and you can post it to him in a nice envelope smelling of roses. Then we'll wait and see what happens."

Mandy seemed on the verge of convulsions again.

"I've just had a brilliant idea," she giggled.

"I'm relieved to hear it. I thought your brain had seized up completely."

"It had for a moment," she admitted. "I wasn't expecting quite such a response."

"What's your brilliant idea, then?"

"Well," said Mandy, glancing at the letter again. "I see that Lulu has promised to send a member of the sales team to interview this gentleman. I know just the person."

"You do?" said Guy, perking up.

"Yes. We Navy wives run an amateur dramatic society. We're sort of resting at the moment and need something to keep us occupied."

"A pantomime, perhaps?"

"More of a one-woman show," Mandy replied.

"With you in the spotlight, I presume?"

"Not on this occasion, ducky. But I'm sure Sue would love to play the part."

"Who's Sue?"

"The bosun's wife. She's a bit of a whore at the best of times and this would be right up her street. She wouldn't even have to dress up."

It was Guy's turn to laugh. Once again, the customers turned their heads to glance at the couple in the corner. If this was supposed to be a discreet meeting to plot the downfall of the Neighbourhood Watch, it had failed completely.

"You're not so dumb, after all," he said. "That would really put the icing on the cake."

"Or the fat in the fire."

Guy gazed fondly at his fellow conspirator. Just the sort of woman he would have liked to marry. Witty, attractive and intelligent. But also sensitive and vulnerable, probably lacking self-confidence because of the ugly scar on her leg.

"It's just as well I'm not a conman," he said.

"Why?"

"Because you'd have swallowed the bait, hook, line and sinker. You should not believe everything you read."

"Fortunately, you are here to protect me."

They finished their coffee and Guy said: "Okay. You have a word with Sue and I'll run off a fair copy. Then you can post it to our friend across the foyer. First class, by the way. Lulu runs a stylish show."

They left the cafe and said goodbye on the pavement. They shook hands and went their separate ways. Too many people had seen them enjoying each other's company to risk an embrace. Despite their collaboration, she was still another man's wife.

Chapter XXII

The Rhône, according to those who lived along its banks, was one the great rivers of France. The greatest, in their opinion. Not that it could compete with the Nile or the Don or rival the Paraña for the amount of water that flowed under its many bridges. But where history was concerned it was more than a match for any streamlet in Europe. Over the centuries, it had – like the Tiber – foamed with much blood, of Celts, Saxons and Gauls, as well as of outlaws, traitors and patriots. It had also absorbed much cow dung, horse manure and grape juice as it meandered south from Lake Geneva towards the sea. In recent years, as industry displaced agriculture along its banks, it had become the dumping ground for the detritus of civilisation. Millions of bottles, as well as bombs, bullets, beer barrels, old bangers and not a few shopping trolleys, had either sunk into the mud or been washed downstream. Plastic wrappers tossed aside with no thought for the environment also drifted with the current, clogging the famous bridge at Avignon before floating into the Med. The Rhône had also seen its fair share of human bodies.

The latest to be hauled from the water, not far from the village of St. Denis les Bains, was that of a middle-aged white man. He would probably have been written off as yet another drunk or suicide were it not for the fact that he was naked and had clearly been tortured. His back bore the marks of cigarette burns while the nails of two fingers on his right hand were missing. The chief of police had seen enough dead bodies to know that the victim in this case was probably still alive when thrown into the river. Mercifully, the water was cold enough to ensure a quick death.

The chief was nevertheless puzzled. The body could not have been in the water for very long as it had barely begun to decompose. Yet there had been no reports of murder or even of missing persons on his patch. The cigarette burns suggested that the victim may well have been a member of a criminal gang, one that had no compunction about using violence to extract information or enforce discipline. He had better things to do than investigate the death of unknown villains. The fewer criminals there were along his stretch of the river the better he would like it.

"Who found the body?" he asked his deputy.

"The river patrol."

"Then you know what to do."

The deputy knew exactly what to do. He was more than familiar with the routine which was to establish as quickly as possible whether the body was that of a local man or woman. If it wasn't, standard practice (although nowhere was this to be found amongst the countless regulations in the rule book) was to pass the buck without delay. In most cases, the incident was not even recorded unless some busybody got to hear about it and demanded to know what the police were doing to identify the corpse. The chief had enough on his plate without having to waste time checking dental records or taking fingerprints. A gold tooth or a matching print were not going to bring the dead man back to life. The best way to handle the matter was to let the authorities downstream deal with it.

And so it was that under cover of darkness the body of Alfred Neuberger, painter and money launderer, was taken out by the same police launch that had brought him ashore and thrown into the river again. Alfred was allowed to float peacefully downstream until he came to a more congenial resting place. There, after a perfunctory examination and a half-hearted attempt to identify him, he was cremated at public expense and his ashes tipped into the river whence he had come. Any hope of identifying the dead man was now extinct.

In the Swiss village of Klugersdorf, the butcher, the baker and the man who mowed the lawn waited in vain for their customer to return. The mayor gave up peeping through the window and the water and electricity at the chalet were cut off. The furniture gathered dust. Even the woman who had visited Herr Neuberger occasionally was not seen again.

It was almost as though she knew he would not be coming back.

Chapter XXIII

Guy was in optimistic mood as he waited for the curtain to rise on the drama that, if all went well, would put the blackmailer out of business. The letter had been delivered the previous day and Mandy had phoned to say that Sue was on her way. He had never met the bosun's wife and was anxious to see what she looked like. A whore at the best of times, Mandy had said, and he hoped she would live up to her reputation. Sue had jumped at the chance to take centre stage and been primed for the part without being told the full story. As a woman whose own husband spent long weeks at sea, she fully understood the need for discretion. Taking a leaf out of the twitcher's book, Guy installed himself behind the curtains and waited for the show to begin.

The bosun's wife, typecast as a fille de joie, was clearly relishing her role as representative of the Godiva Escort Agency. She wore a two-piece costume of brilliant crimson and a matching hat. The skirt was short and tight, accentuating her buttocks, while the jacket allowed a satisfying view of her ample bosom. Her stockings were of the black, fishnet variety while her shoes (maroon) added two inches to her height. She would not have been out of place in one of those strip joints on the Mexican border.

Guy gasped as her taxi drew up at the gate, wondering what he had let himself in for. Taking a notebook from her bag, she conspicuously checked the address, allowing the twitcher plenty of time to observe her arrival. Then she flounced up the path, leaving a trail of Eau de Lilah in her wake. Guy abandoned his position at the window and hurriedly took up a new one behind the front door, hoping to hear what was said.

The putative escort rang the bell of the flat across the foyer. The twitcher opened the door almost immediately, confirming that he had been expecting her to call. Dishevelled and unshaven, he looked as though he had been on the tiles all night. In fact, since receiving the letter from Lulu he had been in a state of shock, unable to eat or sleep. Sue had been warned that he was a bit of a weirdo but the pitiful being who stood before her was even more repulsive than she had imagined. She smiled disarmingly and tried not to show her dismay.

"Mr Wormald?" she enquired, extending her hand.

"Y. .es," the blackmailer replied, ignoring the paw and cringing at the sight of the fire-breathing strumpet with scarlet lips who towered over him.

"I'm from the Godiva Escort Agency. . ."

"How dare you call on me at home?" he cried. "I'm not interested in your services. Clear off!"

He attempted to shut the door but Sue's foot was already over the threshold. A sales career beckoned.

"But surely you received our letter?" she said, projecting her voice in her best stage manner to ensure that everybody in the building could hear.

"You had no right to send such salacious material through the post," the creep declared angrily. "It was completely unsolicited."

"On the contrary," replied Sue. "We were responding to a note that you sent to one of our girls."

"If I'd have known she was one of your girls, I wouldn't have sent it."

"So, you thought she was the type of girl you would normally pick up in the street, did you?" Sue asked innocently.

"I'm not in the habit of picking up women in the street," the schmuck replied, attempting to remove the foot that was still obstructing the door. "Now, clear off before I call the police."

"The police?"

"Yes. You are soliciting for immoral purposes and if you don't go away I shall have you arrested."

"Come now, m'dear," said Sue, arching her eyebrows and surveying this loathsome figure with all the scorn she could muster. "And what if I show them the letter you wrote to Mrs Scott-Hopkins, threatening to expose her unless she met certain conditions?"

The would-be extortionist was so shaken by the arrival of this mind-blowing hussy that he had forgotten why she was there in the first place. He tried to remember what he had said in his letter to Mandy.

"I'm not threatening anybody," he spluttered, trying once again to close the door. "But we don't want your sort around here. You are bringing the neighbourhood into disrepute."

As they spoke, the middle-aged divorcée who lived on the first floor came down the stairs on her way to the shops. She nodded curtly to her neighbour and looked in wonder at the colourful apparition whose perfume threatened to set off the fire alarm.

"All right, dearie," said Sue, playing to the gallery. "If you don't fancy me, I won't be offended. I'll ask Lulu to send you a real scrubber."

The woman stopped and stared at them in amazement. She could not believe that this repulsive little man had ever gone to bed with a woman, let alone sought the embrace of a tart. Stunned by what she had heard, she hurried on, determined to put as much space between herself and the odd couple as possible.

Sue decided that the script had not much further to run. The object of the exercise was clearly on the verge of tears, possibly a nervous breakdown. She took her foot from the door and prepared to leave, but not before firing a parting shot.

"If you did not intend to register with us, why did you write the letter?" she demanded. "I'll have to tell Lulu that you've been wasting our time. We're in business to make money, Mr Wormald, not cater to the whims of Peeping Toms and perverts."

Mr Wormald could find no words to reply. The attempt to exact revenge had totally backfired. It was, he now realised, a terrible mistake to have written the letter. He had not even seen the woman he was trying to blackmail, only her car. She might have been of the same species as the temptress who had been sent to lead him astray. He gave every indication of being about to pee in his pants again. His mortification was complete.

As she reached the front door, Sue turned and blew him a kiss.

"I don't think you're up to it, anyway," she said.

The twitcher slammed his own door and burst into tears. Why did everybody treat him with contempt? He was only trying to uphold moral values and curb anti-social behaviour. He deserved respect, not derision. He had even dared to hope that one day his efforts might be rewarded with a BEM for services to the community. If Mrs Scott-Hopkins referred him to the police, he would be lucky not to be branded a criminal himself. In any case, he would have to resign from the Neighbourhood Watch. They would probably kick him out, anyway. He should never, ever, have written the letter.

On the other side of the foyer, Guy heard the door close and fell about laughing. Sue had given the performance of her life. Not for one moment did the twitcher suspect he was being put through the mill. He phoned Mandy to tell her the good news.

"Sue has promised to give me a full account, anyway," she said. "Let's hope she put the fear of god into him."

"She sure as hell scared the living daylights out of me. What perfume does she use?"

"I've no idea. Why?"

"The place smells like a brothel – and I haven't got any air freshener."

"Open the window," said Mandy. "You're not in a submarine."

"I suppose I shouldn't have expected much sympathy from a sailor's wife."

"I'll show my gratitude next time we meet."

"When will that be?"

"Soon, I hope."

The following morning, Guy was preparing breakfast – which meant unzipping a banana and pouring some milk over a few cornflakes – when the doorbell rang. He could not imagine who might be calling at this hour. Mandy, champing at the bit, perhaps? He opened the door to find a man standing there.

"Taxi, guv?" the caller said.

"Taxi?" said Guy. "I didn't order a taxi."

"Are you Flat Two?"

"No. Wrong door."

"Sorry, guv."

Guy waited while the driver rang the bell of the flat opposite. The door opened to reveal a chastened twitcher struggling with three suitcases. He was wearing a raincoat that could have done with more than a deep clean and was obviously on the point of departure.

"Not leaving us, I hope?" said Guy, as the noisome creature gave the two largest cases to the driver.

"I can't spend another night under the same roof as a man who consorts with prostitutes," he said.

"It's difficult, I know," said Guy, "but one has to be tolerant. Your lady friends don't bother me."

The twitcher ignored the remark and, picking up the smallest case, closed the door and followed the driver towards the cab.

"You've told the landlord, I assume, and left forwarding address?" said Guy.

The twitcher again chose to ignore him and hurried on. The meter was probably already ticking.

"Bon voyage," Guy called after him. "Remember, there is a tide in the affairs of men . . that mistaken for the flood leads to misery and humiliation. Shakespeare," he added.

He closed the door and then phoned Mandy.

"I don't think he'll bother you again," he said. "He's probably decided that blackmail is not his line."

"Thank you, darling," Mandy replied. "You're wonderful."

"Would you care to put that in writing?"

"No – not after seeing what happens to letters that fall into your hands."

While they were chatting, his cornflakes had gone soggy. Guy threw them away and started afresh. After a cup tea and some toast and marmalade, he phoned the florist and ordered a large bunch of roses for Sue, the Navy's most accomplished actress. They cost a small fortune but she deserved them. Her performance had deprived the Neighbourhood Watch of its most dedicated intruder into the lives of others.

Chapter XXIV

Few tears were shed over the snoop's departure. Most of the other residents were glad to see the back of him. Even the divorcée on the first floor seemed relieved that the man had cut and run.

"I always knew he was a queer fish," she confided when she bumped into Guy on her way to work, "but I didn't realise he was in the habit of hiring prostitutes."

"Oh, yes," Guy assured her. "They used to arrive at all hours of the night and day."

"No wonder he looked such a wreck."

"He was hardly the most prepossessing of souls."

"I suppose I should feel sorry for him, having to pay for what most women are happy to give away."

Oh, God! thought Guy. Not another invitation to taste the fruits of Eros. Women were all the same. Always on the lookout for a bit of nookie. Beware of vidders, Sam Weller had warned. The same might be said of divorcées.

"You must drop in for a cup of tea some time," the spouseless one added as she hurried to catch the train.

The air of freedom was infectious. Stimulated by the knowledge that he was no longer under surveillance, at least on the home front, Guy allowed his imagination free rein. His fingers positively danced over the keyboard, turning out nearly a thousand words in the course of one day. He had not made so much progress since he first gave up journalism and began to write fiction. At this rate, his new book would be in the shops before *The Cartesian triangle* had been removed from the shelves.

He had almost forgotten his trip to Grenoble and the disappointment of not finding the picture he had gone there to see. It probably wasn't the one stolen by the Gestapo, anyway. There must be thousands of paintings that fitted the description of the missing Corelli. The odds against finding it were only slightly better than those of winning the lottery.

But something about the visit didn't add up. He tried to remember the sequence of events between getting off the plane and discovering that Lot 49 had been withdrawn from sale. Was it the unexpected appearance of the man from Switzerland or the short phone call the priest had made? Neither incident struck him as significant at the time although the presence of the artist now seemed more than fortuitous. "I am not a great believer in coincidences," Max had said.

Something else the dead man had said continued to resonate. "We won't quibble over the title," Max had declared, opting for the label bestowed by the artist. Guy tried to remember how Brother Alphonse had referred to the painting when they discussed it in Spain. He had certainly used the word *terracotta* in Grenoble. The priest was clearly thinking more about the painting stolen by the Gestapo than the fanciful one in Guy's book. And why had he been trawling through ads. in the newspaper? He surely had better things to do than spend his time looking for bargains at auction sales. The church was supposed to promote spiritual values, not pander to material ones. Guy decided that when he could find a suitable excuse he would ring the priest in Briançon and gently pump him. His training as a journalist was coming to the fore again, just as it had when he asked Max for evidence of his identity. This time he would make sure he got an answer.

In the meantime, he was spending a couple of days a week at Crosbie, Grimshaw and Snape. The agency had at last grown tired of the pesky client who found fault with everything and resigned the account. There were easier ways to earn a living. Guy was assigned to a series of small, one-off ads. designed to keep the name of various clients in the public eye. More PR than hard sell. Grant, the creative director, had ceased to worry about girls with ceramic potties, real or surreal, and turned his attention to girls with inviting smiles. He was not going to replace them with pictures of tractors or Soviet-style assembly lines simply to appease a lot of ugly old feminists. Scantily-clad models helped to sell products. Besides, he liked looking at them.

And the girls liked posing for photos and seeing themselves in print. They liked the money, too. He saw no point in depriving anyone of pleasure by giving in to the demands of a few sanctimonious boob-bashers who were probably just jealous, anyway.

Guy's own thoughts were constantly hijacked by the dark-skinned beauty who captured the imagination in both *The Cartesian triangle* and the missing Corelli. He was beginning to suspect that her role in the real painting was to distract attention from the pot. There was probably a simple explanation for why Brother Alphonse had referred to it as terracotta, rather than earthenware, but for the moment it eluded him. Terracotta belonged to the real world of Corelli and the Gestapo, not to a work of fiction. The next day, at home in Blackheath, he decided to ring the monk and ask him direct.

He dialled the number and hoped that whoever answered could speak English. After a long ringing tone, a woman, probably the housekeeper, picked up the phone.

"Allo?" she said. "Le Hermitage."

"Bonjour, madame. Est-ce que vous parlez anglais?"

"Oui. Un peu."

"Could I speak to Brother Alphonse, please?"

The woman paused before saying: "Brother Alphonse is not here."

"When will he be back?"

"He not come back."

"I thought he lived there?"

"He did. But he go away."

"Where to?"

"I don't know. He just pack valise and go. That is all I can tell you. Bonjour, Monsieur."

She put down the phone.

Guy was stunned. He tried to think of what might possibly have caused Brother Alphonse to leave. A woman, perhaps? The priest was, by his own admission, not exactly celibate. But that was no reason to quit, unless he and his inamorata planned to live openly together in what the church called sin. For a moment, he contemplated phoning Brother Peter in Montserrat. The Benedictines must surely keep tabs on their members, if only to protect church property. God could not keep an eye on everything, even with the help of CCTV. But if word hadn't reached the monastery that the priest was missing, the curator might jump to the wrong conclusion. Unless, of course, the men in red hats knew why their brother had jumped ship and had already taken steps, beginning with a vow of silence, to protect the Order's reputation. He decided to phone Tanya and seek her advice.

"Guy!" she exclaimed. "How nice to hear from you! I thought you must have emigrated."

"Sorry. I've been rather busy just lately."

"Doing what, I wonder?"

"Oh, this and that."

Did she expect him to blurt out that he had been having it off with the secretary of the literary society?

"How's the book coming along?"

"Slowly," said Guy. "The last one's still driving me up the wall."

He told her about his trip to France and the subsequent disappearance of Brother Alphonse.

"He's probably gone off to the Amazon to plant a few trees," said Tanya.

"He'll have to plant one hell of a lot to make up for all those that have been cut down," said Guy.

"Every little sapling helps."

"I don't suppose he'd last very long in that part of the world, anyway. Priests either fall prey to illegal loggers or lonely women."

"The Amazon's not the only place where women can feel lonely," she said.

"Okay, I get the message. I'm sorry."

"Next time, don't leave it so long before you get in touch," she rebuked him. "Even Rachael has been asking about you."

"Rachael?"

"You promised her your autograph."

"I'll pop one in the post straight away."

"Thank you. To what do I owe the pleasure of our present conversation?"

"I need to speak to Michael, actually."

"Michael?" She sounded hurt. He hadn't phoned for weeks and now just wanted to speak to her husband. "What about?"

"I was wondering how the Russian art scene is shaping up. Anyone planning to cash in on a few fake Corellis?"

"I don't know. But he'll be coming home tomorrow and I'll ask him. Have you heard from Amanda lately?"

The question, thrown in so artlessly, sounded innocuous enough. But he was not going to fall into a trap set by a rival. Tread carefully, Sergeant Matthews had advised. He would.

"Yes," he said, deciding that truth was the best defence. "We had coffee the other day."

"To discuss literature, no doubt?"

"That, and other things."

"Has she shown you her scar yet?"

"I didn't know she had one."

Women. If they weren't sure, they guessed. Female intuition, they called it. A stab in the dark, more likely, followed by a stab in the back.

Guy was at home, relishing his new-found freedom to come and go without being spied upon, when the telephone rang. That extension he had promised himself was becoming a necessity, he decided, as he hurried into the hall to answer it. He had been expecting Michael to phone and was surprised when the caller turned out to be Robert, his agent-cum-publicist. They hadn't spoken for weeks.

"What was the name of that bird you fancied?" Robert asked. "The one last seen in a paddy wagon."

"Are you referring to Miss Kovalski?"

"That's the one. Well, she ain't a copper no more."

"What are you talking about?" asked Guy.

"There's a bit in The Times this morning. Apparently, she has been forced to resign."

"Resign? What for?"

"Reading between the lines, I'd say she'd fallen foul of the Met's anti-corruption unit."

"I can't imagine Miss Kovalski doing anything wrong."

"Can't you? Perhaps it's time you had your eyes tested. The scales need to be removed."

The nub of what the agent was saying suddenly hit him. The woman who had aroused his interest and on whom he had spent so much emotional capital was just another bent copper. That probably explained why Sergeant Matthews and Bellicose Bill were so reticent when asked about her. They must have known she was under investigation. The fuzz always looked after their own. In most cases, they tried to keep the story out of the newspapers.

"Did it say which department she worked for?" Guy asked, recalling the sergeant's mention of a special art squad.

"No, only that she had resigned. Funny how they're never sacked, isn't it? Especially when they reach the rank of detective chief inspector."

"My God! I thought she was just an ordinary blackshirt."

"She probably screwed her way up the ladder," said Robert. "A quickie with the super in a cell unused for the night: that's the best way to ensure promotion. Anyway, I thought I'd give you a ring in case you were still working yourself into a frazzle about her."

"I wrote her off some time ago," Guy ruefully admitted. "Not my type, I'm afraid."

"Found somebody to take her place?"

"A temporary arrangement to oblige a lady, that's all."

"Take care! That sort of arrangement usually has strings attached."

"The lady's already married," Guy said, hoping the agent would not press him for details. "The Times, you say? I must buy a copy."

"Don't waste your money. It's only a small paragraph. I'll let you know if they print any more."

The news took the shine off the high spirits Guy had enjoyed since the twitcher had been sent packing. He had suffered a double whammy. First, Brother Alphonse. Gone away, said the housekeeper. No message, no word of explanation. Not even a postcard from the Vatican. Now Miss Kovalski, tarnished by allegations of corruption. Had she been fiddling the books? Bean counters and Portuguese waiters were not the only ones who couldn't add up. The two incidents left him feeling dejected and out of sorts. He could not even summon the energy to phone Mandy in the hope that she might cheer him up. How could he tell her about Miss Kovalski, anyway?

His thoughts turned to the divorcée upstairs. A sex-starved woman, right on his doorstep, might be just what the doctor ordered. But, as Robert had intimated, an affaire with an unmarried woman could be dangerous. They were inclined to be vengeful when passion cooled and easily persuaded that they had been 'abused'. The prospect of being hauled into court by some money-grubbing lawyer was not one to encourage a casual relationship. That's why Guy preferred the frisson of a liaison with a married woman. He could always fall back on the Cold War formula of mutually assured destruction -- "Do you really want your husband to know?" -- if the affaire turned sour. The threat of exposure was usually enough to spike their guns.

As he contemplated the risks of taking tea with the woman upstairs, the telephone rang. This time the caller was Michael. He sounded excited.

"Remember I told you that one of my clients was gulled over a fake picture?" he asked.

"I hope he hasn't tried to get his money back?"

"He's tried, all right, but the seller seems to have left town."

"I don't think I'd hang around if I'd sold a wealthy Russian a pup."

"This guy's not just a wealthy Russian. He has connections, if you know what I mean."

"I do – but don't spell it out over the telephone."

"Don't worry. The mob couldn't be bothered listening to us. Not when they have a hotline to the Kremlin."

"I gather they have their own telephone network, using a scrambler to thwart the law enforcement agencies."

"Law enforcement agencies? In Russia? You must be joking!"

"Somebody must have arrested all those people rotting in jail."

"Ex-KGB thugs who now call themselves the FSB," said Michael. "Putin's men."

"I guess they have to do as they're told."

"They do if they want to draw their pension. If the Kremlin says kill, they kill. You don't argue with the richest man in the world."

"Reminds me of the good old days of Stalin and Trotsky. Have ice pick, will travel."

"Exactly. Look at Magnitsky, beaten to death while in protective custody. Or Litvinenko, poisoned with polonium. Not forgetting Boris Nemtsov or Anna Politkovskaya, of course. Both of them shot."

"Doesn't sound like a very healthy place in which to do business."

"It isn't," Michael replied. "Anybody who crosses Putin tends to fall down dead. But we all have to earn a living, even the purveyors of counterfeit pictures."

"I suppose," said Guy, "that there couldn't be any connection between your fake picture merchant and the disappearance of my religious friend?"

"Why? Has he gone missing, too?"

"Seems like it. Just packed his bags and scarpered."

"Well, fancy that!" exclaimed Michael. "It's probably just coincidence but you can never be sure when the Mafia is involved."

"You're not suggesting he's one of the mob?"

"Who knows? The Vatican is riddled with corruption."

"I thought the church was the prerogative of P4?"

"Nobody has a monopoly when power and money are at stake. The turf wars are never ending."

"I guess you're right."

"And, don't forget, the family has been around for a long time. It has a finger in a lot of pies. Take the FBI, for instance. For almost half a century it was run by a queer who denied the Mafia even existed."

"Hoover, you mean?"

"Yes. The mob had him by the short and curlies."

"I suppose you could say that's their strength," said Guy. "They're not intimidated by the high and mighty."

"They are the high and mighty," Michael said. "That's why nobody dares touch them."

"Moral cowardice," said Guy.

"Of course. But what can you expect from politicians?" Michael paused before adding: "Tanya said you wanted to speak to me. What about?"

"The trade in post-Soviet graffiti," said Guy. "I was wondering if you'd detected any rumbles of discontent among the cognoscenti, apart from your friend's discovery that some folk operate a no-refund policy?"

"Nothing that would help you track down the lost Corelli, I'm afraid, or find your missing friend," said Michael. "But I'll keep my ears open."

Guy was beginning to think he was flogging a dead horse. *The Cartesian triangle* had brought him nothing but trouble, including two visits from the police. He had not even managed to wring any publicity out of Max's death lest he was somehow implicated in his murder. At this stage of his career, he could do without any suggestion that he was on the wrong side of the law. That could come later, when his reputation was secure.

He thanked Michael and turned his thoughts to the petticoat upstairs. Might it not be more profitable to pursue a real bimbo than waste time on a fictional one who refused to divulge the secret of her earthenware jar?

Chapter XXV

Detective chief inspector Kovalski, late of Scotland Yard (or so the Met. would have us believe) was enjoying a brief respite in the grounds of her rented villa on the Costa Brava. The sun was shining but at this time of year -- late autumn: season of mist (at least in the hills) and vinous fruitfulness -- it was too cool to sit on the beach. For warmth, one had to go south to the Costa del Sol but that was full of *por favors* and criminals on the run. Lucy could do without any more villains at this juncture. Her mind was focussed on just one. With a small drink and her mobile phone on the table at her side, she settled down by the pool to await the arrival of her housemate. In her denim jacket and tattered jeans, she looked like any other British holidaymaker in this part of Spain.

Except that Lucy Kovalski was not just another tourist. She was a police officer hard on the heels of a gang of art dealers and money launderers believed to be connected to the Mafia. Thanks to her knowledge of the fine arts, she was the obvious choice when the Met. at last decided to get to grips with the problem. Coppers able to distinguish between op art and pop art were few and far between. Her expertise, plus her propensity for poking her nose into other people's business, had put her in the fast lane to promotion. She had risen rapidly through the ranks, achieving her present status at a relatively early age. This had not made her any more popular than she was at Dartington where she was perceived as a jumped-up country bumpkin too fond of airing her own opinions.

Lucy was no more enamoured of her critics than they were of her. She saw them as morally ambivalent – arrogant, superior types from the Shires, impressed more by wealth than artistic integrity. The more expensive the picture, the more praise they heaped upon it. From the start, she was nettled by the arbitrary values placed on often-frivolous works of art. How could a painting knocked up in two days be worth millions of pounds? Even George Soros would be hard pushed to make that sort of money. For the price of one Caravaggio, a whole village in rural Poland could have lived in luxury for the rest of their lives.

Lucy came from a good Catholic family that tried, and often failed, to live up to the principles laid down by the Holy Father in Rome. She tried harder than most and, while they washed away their sins once a week, she often had to invent transgressions to keep the priest happy. Her real sins weighed heavily on her conscience and it was perhaps inevitable that she was drawn towards the church.

She had grown up in Devon, surrounded by fields in which even the mice were sleek and picky. Her family had never known what it was like to go hungry. Their relatives in Europe were not so lucky. Long before she was born, a previous generation of Kovalskis had suffered loss and privation at the hands of the enemy. Many of their Jewish friends had been rounded up and their possessions carted away by the Gestapo. The people were sent to one of the concentration camps that had sprung up on Polish soil; the pictures – some said to be quite valuable -- found their way into the homes of high-ranking Nazis. Many had still not been traced. Even at this late stage, Lucy was determined to do what she could to recover them and ensure that justice prevailed.

She heard a car arrive and pull up in the driveway. She listened nervously as a man's footsteps rang out on the stone flags of the villa.

"Is that you, Alphonse?" she called.

Alphonse Schreiber, dressed casually in an open-necked shirt and slacks, walked through the house and into the garden.

"Why? Were you expecting somebody else?" he enquired with a smile.

"I have so many admirers one never knows who might drop in," Lucy responded skittishly. "Would you like a drink?"

"Just a small one," the priest replied, taking a seat on the other side of the table. He looked tired. "Did you manage to fix everything?"

"Of course. I'll show you," she said, getting to her feet.

The German held out his hand to stop her.

"No hurry," he said.

She sat down again and poured him a small glass of sherry from the bottle on the table. He lay back in the autumn sunshine and tried to relax. It had been a long and exhausting drive from Briançon to the Spanish border, all the more so because he had not driven the car – last seen at a chalet in Klugersdorf -- before. He had barely had time to master the controls before setting off for Spain. Along the way, he had stopped at one of the family's garages to have the plates changed. That was simply a precaution in case somebody had reported the vehicle stolen. Not that the late owner would need it again.

Lucy often wished she had not been blessed with such a clear sense of right and wrong. This was one of those times. She recalled her first meeting with the man she was about to betray. Both had been at a summer camp for young Catholics in southern Germany and despite the organisers' best efforts to keep the sexes apart they had managed to see quite a lot of one another. He was a few years older than herself but they had kept in touch, even after he had taken holy orders. It gave her a thrill to think that God's rep. could be tempted by the flesh. Adult female flesh, not that of little boys.

His father had been a colonel in the Stasi, the East German security service dubbed the 'sword and shield' of the state.

"That's how we knew the regime was about to collapse," Alphonse had told her. "He saw which way the wind was blowing."

Like most of the thugs who exercised power in East Germany, Colonel Schreiber had no wish to face justice at the hands of those he had helped to oppress. He decided to flee the Democratic Republic before the retributions began. Lucy was not surprised when his son opted for a religious life. It was, perhaps, a way to absolve the sins of the father. Only much later, after she had joined the police, did she begin to have doubts about the man she had once fancied. It came as a severe shock to discover that he fitted the profile, cobbled together by Interpol, of a man wanted for questioning over the theft of paintings from museums and religious institutions across Europe. While some priests turned to whisky and others to pornography, Alphonse had turned to crime.

Lucy knew at once to whom the profile referred. She was torn between friendship and duty. She opted for duty. She even allowed herself to be painted as corrupt in an effort to get closer to the mob. The police needed evidence if they were to bring the criminals to trial. Lucy set about trying to collect it.

"I thought your friend, Mr Chandler, was going to wreck everything by coming to the sale," the German said.

"Well, it was your own fault," Lucy replied. "You shouldn't have drawn his attention to it."

"I thought a dash of psychology might help to muddy the waters, " said Schreiber. "People seldom point the finger at themselves."

Unless they're psychopaths, thought Lucy.

"You might have given me longer warning," she complained. "I thought I'd never reach Grenoble in time to make an offer."

"At least you got there before Alfred. It would have been very awkward if he'd arrived first and put in a bid."

"Yes. You'd have had to launch a recovery operation. He's probably gone home disappointed."

"More than likely," said Alphonse, relieved that news of his death had obviously not yet reached the public domain. "Where is the picture now?"

"Inside. I'll get it. It nearly ruined me, by the way."

"Don't worry, mein liebling. You'll be reimbursed many times over when we crack the riddle."

"If we crack the riddle."

Lucy went into the villa to fetch the Corelli. She had paid far more than it was worth but it was vital to make an offer the trustees would accept. She did not want it to fall into the hands of a third, possibly unknown, party. Her commander at the Yard told her not to worry; the police could not infiltrate the mob unless they were prepared to spend a bit of money. They even sent one of their technical chaps over to France to help them keep an eye on their investment. The man had swiftly drilled a small hole in the back of the frame, inserted an old-fashioned tracking device and expertly repaired the damaged woodwork. Not even a scratch. A surveillance ploy straight out of MI5's handbook. The police hoped the bug would eventually lead them to the mob's clearing house for stolen pictures -- provided it did so before the battery ran out.

Lucy picked up the Corelli and took it out the pool. She was certain that nobody would ever detect that a bug had been installed.

"So," said the German, propping the painting against the table, "we now have access to the Schulman fortune."

"If your theory is correct," said Lucy.

"According to the archives, it is," Schreiber replied.

"Which archives are you talking about?"

"The Stasi's, of course."

"I thought they'd all been destroyed?"

"Most of them were. My father saw to that. But he also managed to transfer several thousand interesting documents to Moscow before the CIA could get their hands on them. I'm assured they are all in safe custody."

His eyes glistened as he surveyed the picture. This was the painting that had already cost the lives of two of his associates: Alexei Bukharov, who had allowed greed to warp his judgement, and Alfred Neuberger, who was beginning to chafe under the restrictions placed on him by the folks in Moscow. It was just as well they had never met. To have recognised each other in the auction room would really have put the cat among the pigeons.

His gaze focussed on the Roman numerals on the terracotta pot.

"Two, three, seven, one, three," he pronounced. "The key to Aladdin's cave."

"Unless he's changed the lock."

"I'm told he hasn't. But, even if he has, there's nothing that cannot be unravelled or retrieved from the depths of cyberspace."

He drained his glass and got to his feet. He stretched and smiled at his companion. For some reason, Lucy was filled with a sense of foreboding. The vibes were all wrong.

"Just think, you and I are the only people outside the Schulman family who know how to access the vault," he said.

"I'm honoured," Lucy replied.

"And so you should be, my dear. Even the Gestapo were unable to squeeze the number out of him."

"I guess he died taking the secret to the grave."

"Or left it scrawled on a bit of canvas, hoping it would survive the war. A noble sacrifice."

Reaching towards the table, the German casually picked up her mobile phone.

"Such a clever little device," he said, turning it over and examining it closely. "Not only does it allow you to speak to your friends, wherever they are, but pinpoints your location."

With a flick of the wrist, he threw the telephone into the pool. Lucy jumped to her feet.

"What the hell do you think you're playing at?" she demanded as the phone sank out of sight.

"A precautionary measure, that's all," Alphonse replied. "You never know who may be listening. Even your friends at Scotland Yard."

"Ex-friends, thanks to you."

"You're a lying bitch," Schreiber replied, his jaw tightening. "I thought it too good to be true that you had been forced to resign."

Lucy shivered. There was a chill in the air and not just because a cloud had cast a shadow over the pool. The atmosphere had changed and she was alone with a man who might turn nasty.

"I suppose you would have preferred that I was sacked?" she said, trying desperately to retrieve the initiative.

"It's quite irrelevant how you left, my dear. Or how much your employers paid for the Corelli."

He picked up the painting and held it at arm's length.

"Such a delightful young lady," he said. "I can see why the old man was so taken with her. She must have been a good lay, even if she was black. Farewell, my lovely."

Before Lucy could stop him, he brought the painting down sharply on the edge of the table, shattering the frame and leaving the canvas flapping loosely.

"What's got into you, for god's sake?" she cried, taking a step towards him. "Have you gone mad?"

"Perhaps," said Alphonse. "But you yourself told me the painting wasn't worth very much."

"What paintings are?" asked Lucky, now thoroughly frightened.

"Not many, unless they contain a message that points to fortune," said Alphonse. "It's a pity you won't be sharing that fortune, my dear."

"Why not?"

"Because . . "

He lunged towards her and grabbed her by the sleeve of her jacket, twisting her arm behind her back.

". . .because, Miss Kovalski, you are about to leave this world and all the evil people in it."

Lucy realised too late that the man of whom she was once very fond was planning to kill her. How she wished she had not turned down the chance to carry a gun. She kicked and struggled, screaming for help, but to no avail. Her police training was no match for brute force. The priest was a big man and extremely powerful. In any case, the neighbours were too far away to hear her cries and even if they did probably would not take any notice. People, especially women, often screamed when they were about to be thrown into the pool. It was part of the holiday ritual. He dragged her towards the pool, taking care not to bruise her, and flung her into the water.

As she floundered, weighed down by her wet clothes, the German stripped off his shirt, kicked off his shoes and jumped in after her. He seized her by the hair and, as she gasped for air, pushed her head under the water. Then, forcing her to the bottom of the pool, he held her down with his feet – he could feel her scratching his ankles -- until he was sure she had stopped breathing. It was a pity she had to die but she really ought not have tried to penetrate the Mafia.

To the world beyond the Costa Brava, it appeared that Detective Chief Inspector Lucy Kovalski, late of Scotland Yard, had fallen into the pool at her rented villa at Lloret del Mar and drowned. Probably after imbibing too much alcohol. Drunken Brits had long given the place bad name.

Alphonse Schreiber hauled himself out of the pool and hurried into the house to find a towel. He was shivering with both cold and emotion. He also had an erection, the natural consequence of grappling with a woman. He did not enjoy killing people but when the family said jump, you jumped. It was either you or the victim. Alphonse wanted to live for a while yet, preferably in comfort. Thanks to the girl with the terracotta pot, he now had the means to ensure that comfort.

After changing his clothes and a quick drink to calm himself, he fell to his knees and prayed for the soul of the woman he had just murdered. He no longer believed in God but, to be on the safe side, he also sought absolution for himself. If God did exist, he would surely forgive. Then, donning a pair of rubber gloves, he returned to the pool and began to pervert the course of justice.

Taking the bottle of sherry, he carefully filled her glass, then knocked it over, watching the pale yellow liquid spread across the table. Despite the inevitable evaporation, the stain would still be there in a couple of days. He removed his own glass, washed it carefully and put it back in the cupboard. Then he collected the pieces of the wrecked Corelli, including the bug placed so skilfully by Scotland Yard, put them in a plastic bag and transferred them to the boot of his newly-acquired car.

As a German, he was nothing if not thorough. Searching the villa until he found a vacuum cleaner, he carefully hoovered around the table to remove any small piece of evidence that might fall into the hands of the Spanish police. He did not have much faith in them – they lacked the forensic skill of the Yard -- but it was best not to take any chances. Tipping both evidence and dust into another bag, he put that in the boot, too. Then he stood back and drew a deep breath.

The body of the woman who had got too close for comfort was still lying at the bottom of the pool. The maid would find it when she arrived to clean the villa at the end of the week. By then, it would probably have floated to the surface. The overturned glass would suggest that the dead woman had been drinking and had probably slipped and fallen into the water. By the time the police arrived, Alphonse would be well on the way to Malta. It would be a pity to abandon the car but that couldn't be helped. He might perhaps arrange for the previous owner, who had been forced to let it go for much less than market value, to travel to Spain and collect it. He deserved a reward for all his efforts on behalf of the family. He had even managed to sell a counterfeit picture to one of their own in Moscow.

He wondered whether to leave a note suggesting that Inspector Kovalski had taken her own life after losing her job. But, thanks to an informer at the Yard, he knew she had not been sacked and that the story which had appeared in the papers was a bum steer. It had probably been placed by a high-up in the commissioner's office who had a friend in Fleet Street. Besides, a note would belie the scene he had so carefully contrived at the edge of the pool. Better to let things stand. The coroner would almost certainly bring in a verdict of accidental death. She would not be the first Brit to drown in a Spanish swimming pool, probably after drinking too much. Her superiors at the Yard might know that she never drank to excess but the Spanish coroner wouldn't.

Taking his time, the Mafia's man in the Rhône valley removed his few items of clothing from the wardrobe and packed them carefully in his bag. He had plenty of time – the maid would not be there for at least forty-eight hours -- and to rush would risk making a mistake. The mob did not make mistakes. That, coupled with a little violence now and again, was how they managed to stay in business. When he was satisfied there was nothing to indicate that he had ever been in the house, he put the bag on the back seat of Alfred's motor car and drove south to Alicante, stopping occasionally to throw out a piece of the painting whose secret had at last been revealed. The dust he disposed of in a bin in a small town along the way. Then he abandoned the car, caught a bus to the airport and bought a ticket to Malta. He liked to be near the money, especially when dealing with Russians. All too often, it tended to disappear when entrusted to their care. The attempt to access the Schulman family vault could come later, when the dust had settled.

Back in London, the Met. wondered why an ostensibly valuable painting had been left on the side of a road, a few miles south of Tarragona. Its plaintive bleeps were akin to a distress signal. The man who had planted the bug was sent to investigate.

Her colleagues at the Yard were also becoming increasingly concerned about the fate of DCI Kovalski. Her phone had stopped working and they had not heard from her for several days.

They would never hear from her again.

Chapter XXVI

The funeral was a dry-eyed affair. The Spanish authorities had held on to the body until they were satisfied there had been no foul play. By the time they released it, the initial shock of her death had been absorbed and grief had given way to a subdued sense of loss.

Guy was among the handful of mourners who gathered on a cold winter's day at St. Agatha's Catholic church in North London, not far from where she lived. She had apparently gone to mass there. Others who came to pay their respects included one or two friends and colleagues from the Yard. Sergeant Matthews, looking sombre in a dark suit and black tie, was among them. Two senior officers in dress uniform added a touch of gravitas. The police had been unable to track down her next of kin, named as a sister in America, and had been left holding the baby. They had arranged for the body to be flown back to England and, as she had died on duty, even paid for the funeral. That DCI Kovalski had allegedly been sacked for corruption was conveniently overlooked.

Guy had phoned the Lopatas in Devon to break the news. They expressed their condolences but declined to make the journey to London. The cows still had to be milked and the fare was prohibitively expensive. And, as Chris Lopata had pointed out, he was not exactly wowed by the girl from Dartmoor. They sent some flowers, anyway.

Guy was saddened by her death. He had been smitten, no doubt about it, but their stars had never aligned. Fate had decreed that romance was not to be. His agent had phoned him early one morning to break the news gently before Guy could read about it in the papers. The death of Chief Inspector Kovalski was splashed across all the inside pages, not just in The Times. According to the coroner, Robert said, she had fallen into the pool after drinking too much. Guy thought that was rather odd. He remembered the first time they had met, at the reception to launch *The Cartesian triangle*. She had barely touched her wine, unlike the critics who had turned up for a free tipple to help them digest the prose. A good review often depended on the flow – and quality -- of the wine. But if the coroner said she had drowned while under the influence he couldn't argue. He wasn't there.

The maid had been questioned but the poor woman was too distraught to give a coherent account. She had met the deceased only once but said that she seemed a nice woman. Hardly the sort, well, the sort of holidaymaker she'd often had to clean up after on the coast. She agreed that it was a big house for one person but insisted that she had not seen anyone else there. The English lady liked big houses, perhaps, and maybe friends would join her later. The coroner wanted facts, not conjecture, and discharged her. Verdict: accidental death. If the British wanted to hold their own inquest, that was their affair. Next, please.

Guy shivered as the requiem continued. It was cold in the church and there were not enough mourners to generate much heat. He could have done with a hot-water bottle. The priest cast a spell over the body and mumbled a few words to speed the soul on the way to heaven. With that, the funeral was over. There were others in the queue, waiting for St. Peter to open the Pearly Gates. Lucy was carted away to the crematorium where the air was much warmer. Quite hot, even. RIP.

As he was leaving the church, Guy felt a friendly hand on his shoulder. He turned to see Sergeant Matthews. The copper looked vaguely embarrassed.

"I thought I'd better just put the record straight," he said. "I knew who Lucy was, of course, but couldn't tell you. There are some things the police can't admit for operational reasons."

"I quite understand," said Guy. "Did you know her well?"

"Only as a colleague," the sergeant said. "She always struck me as a bit standoffish but she knew her stuff. She would have gone a long way."

"But not to get a drink," said Guy.

The sergeant gave him a knowing look.

"That was my impression, too," he said. "In fact, she was almost teetotal. She wouldn't even raise a glass at the Christmas party."

"Strange that she should fall into the pool after drinking too much."

"Very strange. But if that's what the coroner said . . " The detective shrugged. "Can I give you a lift? The car's just down the road."

Guy thanked the sergeant but declined the offer and decided to make his own way back to the City.

Sitting on the top deck as the bus threaded its way through the traffic, he reflected on the events of the past few months. The Grim Reaper had been constantly at his side. First Max, shot dead as he walked down the street. Guy wished he had asked the sergeant how the murder enquiry was going. Now Miss Kovalski had departed for the infinite custody suite in the sky. He wondered whether her death was also linked to his book, as Max's appeared to have been. Then there was Brother Alphonse. Not dead, as far as he knew, but missing in action.

It occurred to him that Lloret del Mar was not far from Figueras where he had first met the priest. Nor was it a million miles from Montserrat, whose monastery boasted a fine collection of paintings. Was it just coincidence that Miss Kovalski . . no, the thought was too fantastic. A successful heist would require a great deal of planning and inside information. More than one visit would have been necessary for the priest to suss out all the security arrangements. Now that he appeared to have abandoned his calling, he would no longer be welcome, anyway.

As the bus neared his destination, Guy rang the bell and got off.

He had almost finished his new book, which was just as well. He needed to earn some money. His work at the agency had dried up and once again the wolf was prowling around the door. With any luck he could screw a reasonable advance out of the publisher. That, in addition to royalties from *The Cartesian triangle,* would keep him nourished until Spring. But then what? He would cross that bridge when he came to it. The world might have split asunder by then, riven by the occupant of the White House or by some new superbug. In the meantime, life had to go on.

One morning, as he sat huddled over his computer putting the finishing touches to the manuscript, the doorbell rang. He pushed the keyboard to one side and went to investigate. He was astonished to find Rachael, Tanya's daughter, standing there. She had a large painting under one arm and looked older and more sophisticated than when they had first met. She had obviously been at her mother's perfume and was not there to discuss the Holocaust.

"Hullo," she said. "May I come in?"

The end

Printed in Great Britain
by Amazon

40320856R00112